Jacob Abbott

John Gay

Work for Boys

Jacob Abbott

John Gay
Work for Boys

ISBN/EAN: 9783337400408

Printed in Europe, USA, Canada, Australia, Japan

Cover: Foto ©Andreas Hilbeck / pixelio.de

More available books at **www.hansebooks.com**

JOHN GAY; OR, WORK FOR BOYS.

By JACOB ABBOTT.

IN FOUR VOLUMES.

ILLUSTRATED BY H. W. HERRICK.

WORK FOR SUMMER.

NEW YORK:

PUBLISHED BY HURD AND HOUGHTON,

401 BROADWAY, COR. OF WALKER STREET.

1864.

CONTENTS.

ENGRAVINGS.

JOHN GAY'S WORK IN SUMMER.

CHAPTER I.

JOHN'S GREENBACKS.

IN the back yard belonging to the house
where John and Benny lived, there was a
pump not far from the kitchen-door, with
a wooden platform leading out to it from
the door. Before the pump there was a
spout, of the kind which the carpenters
call a shoe, made to catch the waste water,
and convey it into an opening in the
ground, where there was a grating through
which it flowed into a dark recess in the
earth, that led away, Benny could never
imagine where.

Benny used to try to sail boats by means
of the water from this pump, but it troubled
him a good deal to get a pond large
enough. Sometimes he would borrow a
large tin milk - pan from Bridget in the
kitchen, and contrive to block it up level

under the nose of the pump, and then pump it full of water, and sail his boats in that.

At last, one day, it occurred to · John that he might make Benny a somewhat larger pond, by using the spout itself for this purpose. The spout was pretty wide at the back end, and was about two feet long. It was laid upon the platform of the pump, and made to slope downward somewhat, so as to carry off the water. The back end, and the two sides of the spout, were enclosed by means of narrow pieces of board nailed on to them, but the lower end was left open to allow the water to flow out.

John contrived to block up this lower end with a piece of wood placed under it, so as to make it level, and then to make a kind of dam across the opening by means of a short board, which he cut as nearly as possible to the right dimensions, and then filled in the interstices with clay, so as to make it nearly water-tight.

" There, Benny," said John, " now you can pump that full of water, and you will have quite a large pond. And now I think you ought to pay me for doing this work. for you."

" Well," said Benny, " I would pay you if I only had some money."

" You can pay me in work," said John.

" Well," replied Benny, " I will be your apprentice."

" No," said John; "apprentices are never paid for their work, — only journey-men."

" What is a journeyman?" asked Benny.

" He is a man that has learned how to work at his trade," replied John, " and so the master pays him for what he does. When he is an apprentice, he does not know enough to work for pay; so he only works for his teaching and his board. If you are going to work for pay, you will be a journeyman."

" But I am not going to work for pay," said Benny. " I am going to work to pay you."

" Oh, that's the same thing," said John. " You are going to work for pay, and your pay is this pond, only I have paid you in advance."

Benny was a little confused at these

various distinctions about pay, and after a
moment's pause he said, —

"Well, I will be your journeyman.
What will be the work for me to do?"

"Wheeling off the weeds from my garden," said John. "I am weeding out my
garden, and I shall want you to rake up
the weeds as fast as I throw them out, and
wheel them away to the compost-heap."

"I don't like to wheel weeds," said Benny, beginning to look rather out of hu-
mor.

"But if you are my journeyman," said
John, "you must do just what I say.
That is always the way with journeymen."

"Then I won't be your journeyman at
all," said Benny.

"Then you can't have this pond," said
John.

Benny looked down at the pond, which
he had in the mean time pumped full of
water, and appeared to be very much dis-
turbed in mind at the idea of losing it.

"I can take the dam away," said John,
"and let the water all run out again, if
you are not willing to pay for it."

It was certainly right that Benny should

do what he could to recompense John for
the time and pains he had taken to make
his pond; and it was only strict justice that,
if he was not willing to do this, he should
not have the pond.

But strict justice is not the proper thing
to be dealt out to such a little boy as Benny by an older brother. Generosity is very
much better.

" On the whole," said John, after a moment's reflection, " I believe I will let you
have this pond for nothing. And after this,
when you want me to do anything for you,
you must be my journeyman, and work
for me first; and then I will pay you with
some kind of money, and you must keep
the money; and, when you want me to do
anything for you, you must pay me."

"What kind of money shall you pay
me ? " asked Benny.

" I will make some money in my shop,"
said John. " I'll go and do it now, while
you stay here and sail your boats in your
new pond."

So John left Benny sailing the boats,
and went into the shop. Here he took a
long and slender strip of wood, and planed

it out very thin, — as thin as a common
book-cover. The piece was about three
fourths of an inch wide. This piece he
divided, by means of his compasses, into
parts an inch and a half long, and then
with the fine saw he sawed through at each
division. Thus he had about a dozen ob-
long pieces, very thin, and somewhat of the
shape of bank-bills. He said to himself
that he was going to make greenbacks of
them, by painting the backs of them green.

He determined to have five denomina-
tions of this money, — ones, twos, threes,
fives, and tens; and he marked the number
denoting the denomination on each piece
with a very narrow chisel, thus, I, II, III,
V, X. As he had twelve pieces in all,
he found he could make four of each denomination.

By the time that he had proceeded thus
far with his work, Benny came into the
shop to see what he was doing. He was
very much pleased with the looks of the
money, and said that he wished that John
would give him some work to do at once,
so as to pay him some of the money.

"No," said John; "the money is not

ready to be issued yet. It is not finished."

Benny wished to know what else was to be done to the pieces.

" I am going to make greenbacks of them," said John ; " I am going to do it this evening, when we go in the house. But you can work if you choose, provided you will trust me to pay you when the money is done."

Benny said he was willing to do this, and John told him that the price he should pay him for his work would be a dollar an hour.

" But you will have to pay *me two* dollars an hour," he added, " for *my* work."

" Ah, no, John," said Benny, " that would not be fair."

" Yes," said John, " for I can do as much for you in one hour as you can do for me in two. Because you see that I am older and stronger than you are ; and besides, I work with tools for you, to make boats and such things. It is always worth more to work with tools."

But Benny could not be convinced that John's work was worth twice as much as his, and finally they agreed upon what the lawyers call a reference; that is, they both said that they would leave it to their mother to decide.

"You must not tell her what you think," said John, "and I will not tell her what I think. We will only ask her how much she thinks an hour of work that you do for me is worth, paid in work that I do for you, — that is, how much more my work is worth than yours."

"Yes," said Benny.

"And will you abide by what she says?"

"Yes," said Benny; "if she says your work is worth twice as much as mine, I will agree to it."

During all the time that the boys had been talking in this way, John had been continuing his work upon his money. He rubbed each of the pieces upon fine sand-paper, so as to smooth the edges and the sides, and make them all perfectly nice and clean. Benny helped at this work as well as he could, standing upon the platform which John had made for him to bring him up to the proper height.

"John," said Benny, "you have not

made money enough. I mean to do a great deal more work than this will come to."

" Yes," said John, " but this same money will do over and over again. You see, first I shall pay you with it for your work, and then pretty soon you will come and bring it to me to pay me for mine. Then I shall have it again to pay you; and so it will be going back and forth all the time, and in the end will pay for twenty times as much work as the money itself comes to."

Benny was somewhat puzzled with this idea of being paid over and over again for his work, by the same money, — but wiser heads than his have been puzzled before with the mysterious principles which regulate the flux and reflux of a circulating medium, in its going out from and returning to the issuer of it.

So, after standing still a moment, lost in perplexity, he gave up the attempt to understand the subject, and went on rubbing the pieces of money with the sand-paper more briskly than ever.

By the time that the pieces were all nicely smoothed, and wiped with a cloth

clean from the dust which the sand-paper
had made, the bell rang for supper, and the
boys went in.

That evening after supper the boys went
to their desk in the sitting-room, and there
John, taking out his box of paints, rubbed
some pretty green paint, and painted the
backs of all his bills of a bright green.
After the first coat was dry, he put on another, so as to have the wood perfectly covered.   He then painted the edges of each
piece of a bright red, and also carried a narrow stripe of red all around the margin on
the front side, too.

As fast as John finished the painting of
the pieces, he laid them down carefully,
charging Benny not to touch them.

" May I touch them when they are dry ? "
asked Benny.

" No," said John ; " you must not touch
them till the colors are *fixed.*"

" How are you going to fix them ? " asked
Benny.

" With boiled linseed oil," said John.

But I must postpone explaining how
John was going to do this until the next
chapter.

CHAPTER II.

FIXING THE COLORS.

ONE of the most important, and at the same time most delicate of the operations connected with the manufacture of the real greenbacks, is to *fix* the colors, — that is, to make them permanent and indelible, so that they will not fade out or wear off by use, and cannot be effaced or altered by counterfeiters. And John's wooden green-backs were in this respect like the genuine ones. It was necessary to *fix* the colors. John did this by varnishing them over, after he had put on the green and the red in water, with *boiled linseed oil.*

It is much more easy and convenient to paint in water-colors — that is, in colors mixed with water — than with oil-colors, which are colors mixed in oil; but with oil-colors the work is a great deal more secure and durable; for the oil, when it becomes dry and hard, holds the color so that water will not take it off. The oil that is used must be what is called a drying oil, that is, one of the kind that becomes *hard* and *dry* on exposure to the air. The kind which is generally used for this purpose is called boiled linseed oil, and it can be bought at any painter's.

The paints that are used by painters are mixed with this, or some other kind of drying oil, but it is very inconvenient and troublesome to use it; for water will not wash it off, but it will stick and stay wherever it touches; though it can be washed off when it is fresh, and before it has had time to dry, by means of soap, and even after it is somewhat dry, by spirits of turpentine.

It is so troublesome to do this, that instead of washing their brushes when they wish to change from one color to another, painters generally have a separate brush for every separate color, and this would be very inconvenient for children.

But there is a way of combining the advantages of both methods; and that is by putting on the colors first with water, and then, when the water has dried off, washing them over with oil. This, as it were, makes oil-colors of them after they are put on; for the oil soaks in among the particles of color on the wood, and when it hardens it binds them all as firmly together as if they had been put on in oil, and covers the whole surface moreover, above the color, with a thin but hard and permanent coating, like a kind of varnish, which prevents the colors from washing off if they get wet afterward.

For all such purposes, therefore, as John's, in the making of his greenbacks, the best way for boys who are old enough and careful enough to be intrusted with oil in any form, is to put on the colors first in water, from a common paint-box, and then afterward fix them by applying a coat of oil.

Varnish is still better, for it gives the wood or the substance, whatever it is that is painted, a fine glossy surface; but varnish is more expensive than oil.

John painted his greenbacks, as has already been said, in the house in the evening, and left them there on his desk to dry. The next morning he and Benny, taking them up carefully, carried them out to the shop to be oiled.

2

He kept his bottle of oil on the lower shelf of the cupboard at the end of his bench, and the brush by the side of it. This brush was one that once belonged to a bottle of mucilage, and when the mucilage was used out, John had saved the brush; and, after soaking it in water all one night to dissolve off the hardened mucilage, he washed it clean the next morning, and it made an excellent brush for his oil. He washed it carefully too, with soap, every time that he used it, so that it never became stiff and hard, but was always in good order for use.

The bottle, too, and the cork which stopped the mouth of it, were always clean and in good order; for John always wiped out the mouth of the bottle with a rag, after he had been using it, before he put the cork in, and he also, in the beginning, rubbed a very little tallow on the cork, which not only helped to keep the air from penetrating through the interstices around it, and so hardening the oil inside, but also made it go in and come out easily.

You will perhaps guess that the person who taught him all these things was Ebenezer; but you are mistaken if you do, as will appear presently.

John brought out the greenbacks and laid them down carefully on a smooth board upon his bench, and then took out his oil and his brush. Then he paused and seemed to be lost in thought.

" What is it ? " asked Benny.

" I am thinking," said John.

" What are you thinking about ? " asked Benny.

" I am thinking whether I had better oil my greenbacks with my brush or with a rag. It is nicer to do it with the brush ; but then I have the trouble of washing the brush afterward. But if I take a rag, then when I have done I throw the rag away. So when I have only a *little* oiling to do, I generally take a rag, — one of those."

So saying, John pointed to a little shelf which he had made against the wall opposite to his bench, on which lay a little pile of cotton rags, about two inches square each, which he had prepared by tearing up some large pieces of cotton cloth that his mother had given him out of her rag-bag.

John used these rags for various purposes

— such as oiling any small thing that he had made; as, for instance, a handle for some little tool, or an arrow for Benny, or a silk-winder for his mother. All these things look much better when oiled, as by that means the colors of the wood, whether it be pine, mahogany, birch, or any of the more valuable fancy woods, are brought out by the oil, and made to look much prettier Then, besides, the surface, when thus oiled, becomes hard and impervious to water, so that the piece does not take a stain so easily, and thus keeps cleaner and nicer under use.

John also used his little rags to wipe his tools with, when he whetted them on his oil-stone, and to wipe out the mouth of his oil-bottle before he put the cork in, after using it, and for many other purposes. He called them his towels.

" On the whole," said John, after pausing for a moment to consider whether he should use his brush or a little towel, to oil his greenbacks, " I think it will be better to take the brush. That will be the *best* way, and Ebenezer says, ' Do what you do in the very best way, — no matter for the trouble.' "

John had a little saucer, which I think must have once belonged to a doll's tea-set, for it was not bigger round than the palm of his hand, and so could not have been intended to be used by real people. Besides, his cousin Mary gave it to him, and it probably belonged to a set which she had when she was a little girl. He took this saucer and poured out a few drops of the oil into it, taking care to turn the bottle round, and cant it over backward when he had done pouring, so as to let the drop that remained on the lip flow back into the bottle, instead of running down outside.

It was not Ebenezer, as has been intimated once before, that taught John such niceties as these. Ebenezer was extremely precise and particular about all substantial things, and about everything that concerned the rapid and perfect completion of his work ; but he paid no attention to those little niceties in respect to the modes of doing it, which are very important for a gentleman to observe, who undertakes to amuse himself with mechanical operations. It was John's uncle Edward who taught him things of this kind.

Ebenezer would have considered it very small business to make up a parcel of little towels to wipe his tools with. He used to reach out upon his bench and take up a handful of shavings, wherever he saw them, for this purpose, and then throw them down upon the floor. And when he poured oil out of his oil-bottle he paid very little attention to the drop that was left upon the lip of the glass. The consequence was that in process of time the mouth and neck of the bottle became all gummed over with a mass of hardened oil, like the drippings from a flaring candle, so thick that you could not tell what the original shape of it was at all.

This was all very well for a farmer's shop, and for a workman who always wore a working-dress. The time that is required for doing things nicely would have been thrown away for him. It was different, however, for a young gentleman like Edward, or for a boy like John, who must always keep their dress clean and nice, and who often wish to bring their work into the house, and even into the parlor.

John learned to be so neat and nice in his

work by his practice during the summer, that on the following winter he used often to put his bottle of oil and one of varnish, his brush, his little towels, and his box of paints, all upon a large wooden tray that he made for the purpose, and bring them into the parlor during the long evenings, and there work, in company with Mary and Benny, in making little toys of various kinds, and painting and varnishing them.

" Now, Benny," said John, after he had begun oiling his greenbacks, " go out in the barn and bring me in three or four clean straws. Don't be long choosing them, but come quick. I will count it as a part of your time that I am to pay you for."

Benny ran off to execute this commission. When he returned with the straws, he found that John had already oiled two or three of the greenbacks. John selected two long straws from those which Benny brought, and laid them down pretty near together on the board, and then placed the greenbacks that he had oiled across them.

" What is that for?" asked Benny.

" What do you put the greenbacks on the straws for ? "

" To keep them up off the board," said John, " so that the air can come to them all around and harden the oil."

John proceeded in this way to oil all his greenbacks, and Benny was surprised to find how much it improved the appearance of them. It not only made the painted portions on the back and on the edges look bright and pretty, but it also brought out the color of the wood on the *facing* where it had not been painted, and deepened and darkened it so as to give a finished look to the whole piece. Some of the oil, too, settled in the marks made by the chisel to denote the denomination of the piece, and made them look a great deal plainer.

On the whole, Benny was so much pleased with the appearance of the money that he began to think that, if he should earn some of it, and John should pay him, instead of paying it back to John for work that John was to do for him, he should rather keep it for his own.

" Very well," said John, " you can keep it if you please. When people earn money by their work, they have a right to keep it, or spend it, just as they like."

After the greenbacks were all oiled, John set the board which contained them before the window to dry, and then went to wash his brush. He brought out a cake of brown soap from the kitchen, and then, while Benny pumped, he held the soap and his brush under the stream of water, and when they were wet he rubbed the brush upon the soap until he had made a good lather upon it, working the brush every way so as to make sure that the lather should penetrate among all the bristles.

Then, after rinsing off the brush by letting Benny pump some clean water upon it, he carried the soap back to the kitchen and then returned with Benny to the shop, where he wiped the brush dry with one of his towels, and then put brush and oil-bottle away in their place, all ready to be used another time.

" And now, when will the greenbacks be dry ?" asked Benny.

" To-morrow," said John. " But if you choose you can earn one of them to-day, and I can set it aside on the board and it

will be yours ; only you can't take it away
very well till to-morrow."

"Well," said Benny, "I'll go and get
the wheelbarrow, and wheel away the
weeds."

CHAPTER III.

SUMMER SNOWBALLING.

One day in the early part of June there was a cold rain-storm, and John and Benny, after playing for some time in the barn and sheds, and doing a little work in John's shop, came into the house and proceeded to the sitting-room, where they found their mother sitting by a small fire which had been made there.

"Mother," said John, "it is as cold as winter. All your plants in the garden will freeze."

"No," said his mother, "nothing can freeze to-day. The cold is not down to thirty-two; and nothing freezes till the thermometer goes down to thirty-two."

"But, mother, you don't know but that it *is* down to thirty-two to-day. You don't know how cold it is!"

"But I know it is not so cold as thirty-two," replied Mrs. Gay, "because it is *rain*,

and not *hail* or *snow* that comes down from
the air, and the rain does not freeze when it
gets to the ground.   That shows that neither the air nor the ground are as low as
thirty-two, for that is where freezing always begins."

"At any rate, it is too cold to stay out
any longer," said John, "and we have not
got anything to do in the house."

"How would it do for you to play that
it is winter, and so you and Benny have a
snowballing?"

"But, mother," said John, "we have not
got any snow to make our balls of."

"You can make snowballs out of old
newspapers," said Mrs. Gay.

"So we can, Benny," said John. "Come
out into the back hall, and we will have a
combat."

So John and Benny went out to the back
hall and began at once to make up snowballs out of some old newspapers that their
mother gave them from a closet.   They
made their balls about as big as the real
snowballs ordinarily made by boys.   It
took nearly a quarter of a newspaper for
each ball, they were so large.   They made

them by crumpling the paper up and crowding it together in their hands until it was
sufficiently round and solid to be thrown.

John then contrived a game as follows :
One was to take one end of the hall and
one the other, and then they were to fight
their battle by throwing the balls at each
other. They only made about a dozen
balls, knowing that after the battle began
they could pick up the balls as they fell,
and use them over again a great many
times.

Now, a make - believe battle is a very
amusing play for boys, but it is usually a
very unsafe one ; for, however good-na-
turedly and playfully it may be begun, it
is very apt to result in serious earnest, and
so end at last in angry blows, and cries of
vexation and pain. John, however, who
was a very ingenious boy in all things,
always displayed a great deal of tact in
contriving ways of guarding against these
dangers in his plays with Benny, and with
other little boys. The plan that he contrived
in the case of this snowballing was this.

" Now, first, Benny," said he, " we will
draw the bounds. We will make a line

across the floor, in the middle, and you
shall have one end of the hall and I will
have the other."

"Well," said Benny, "make a mark with
a piece of chalk."

"No," said John; "I will lay down a
piece of twine. That will do just as well,
and it will be easier to take up the twine,
after we have done playing, than to rub out
the chalk-mark."

So John drew out a piece of twine from
his pocket, and laid it down across the floor,
so as to divide the hall into two nearly
equal parts.

"And I must have this side," said Benny, pointing, "because I want the stairs
for my fort."

"Very well," said John. "You shall
have that side and I will take this. You
shall have six of the balls and I will have
six.

"And we will count the hittings," continued John, "and whoever hits the most,
beats. We will have ten hittings for the
game. Whichever of us hits the other ten
times first, beats, and shall have the prize.
We must have something for the prize."

John decided to have lumps of sugar for the prize, if his mother would give him some. So he went to her and asked her. She said she was very willing to give him some sugar, and she selected half a dozen lumps, each one about as big as a bean.

John carried these lumps back to the hall, and then arranged that the prize for each game should be two lumps of sugar. Whoever conquered was to have both these lumps, on condition, however, that he gave one of them to the boy that was beaten.

It was very thoughtful and considerate in John to make this arrangement; for otherwise, if he should beat Benny, as he thought it highly probable he often would, Benny would have, in addition to the mortification of being beaten, the chagrin and vexation of seeing John eating a lump of sugar, while he had none himself. It is true John might in such a case *give* Benny a part of the prize ; but he knew very well that it would not afford Benny nearly as much satisfaction to receive it in that way, as it would to have it come to him in his own right, through the regular operation of the game.

Things being thus arranged, John laid down the two lumps of sugar, which were to constitute the first prize, upon the table before the window, and the battle began.

John hit Benny twice before Benny could hit him once. Benny seemed to feel somewhat discouraged when he was struck the second time, and he held up his hand for a parley.

"John," said he, "it is not fair to count yours and mine the same. You are older than I am, and so you can hit me oftener."

"But then," said John, "remember that I am a great deal bigger than you are, and so I am much easier to hit than you. So that one thing balances the other. My bigness as a mark makes up to you for my bigness in throwing. And then, on your part, if you are little to throw, you are also a little thing to hit."

"I am *not* a little thing," said Benny, in quite an indignant tone.

"No," said John; "I was wrong in that, for you are growing to be a pretty big boy. But then you are not so big to hit as I am."

Benny was somewhat soothed in his

feelings by this apology, but he was by no means satisfied with John's reasoning.

" No," said Benny, " that is not fair. Besides, you said in our work that one hour of what you did should go for two hours of mine, and it ought to be so in this play. One of my hits must count two of yours."

" But you did not agree to that," said John.

" No," said Benny; " we were going to leave it to mother."

" So we were," said John; " but we never did. Let's go now."

" Well," said Benny, " we will. I am sure she will say that one of my hits ought to count for two of yours; — or else you will get all the sugar."

So the boys threw down the snowballs that they had in their hands, and went into the sitting-room to see their mother and refer the question of the comparative value of the performances of the two boys, both in relation to work and play.

It had been agreed that the question should be stated fairly to their mother, and without giving her any clue to what the

3

boys themselves severally thought in relation to it.   John did state the question very
fairly as follows : —

"Mother," said he, "Benny and I want
to know how his time and mine ought to
be reckoned, when we work for each other.
That is, when he works for me an hour,
how much ought I to work for him to pay
him.   Is that a fair way to ask her?"
added John, turning to Benny.

"Yes," said Benny, "that's fair.   I
think "—

"No," said John, "stop.   You are not
to tell mother what you think, and I am
not to tell her what I think, but only ask
her the question."

"Well, let me see," said Mrs. Gay.
"That is rather a difficult question.   Are
you going to make any bargains that will
depend upon my answer?"

"Yes, mother," said John.   "He is going
to pay me for what I do for him, and I am
going to pay him for what he does for
me."

"And so I am to set an estimate upon
the comparative value of your labors," rejoined Mrs. Gay, "for you to arrange the

bargain by it. That is a serious question, and rather a difficult one. Go back to your play for awhile, and I will think about it, and tell you by and by."

" Yes, Benny," said John, " we will go back and I will let it be just as you said, until mother gives her decision."

So the boys went back, and resumed their battles, on the understanding that two of John's hits should only count for one of Benny's. But John found that even at that rate he was likely to win the game very soon, for notwithstanding all Benny's hiding behind the stove, and running up the stairs, he got hit quite often, while he could seldom hit John at all. So, finally, John managed his firing in such a way as to come as near to Benny as he could without hitting, and to expose himself freely to Benny's shots. He thus had the magnanimity to allow Benny to beat him, at almost every game, and to have the pleasure of taking the prizes, — though he always gave one of the lumps of sugar to John, according to the rule which had been established at the outset.

The boys played five or six games in

this way, and they warmed themselves so
effectually by the exercise that they made
no more complaints about the weather
being cold. When they were tired of
playing, they gathered all the snowballs up,
and put them away in a basket, ready
for another game with them the next cold
day.

.

CHAPTER IV.

DUPLICATE RATIO.

When Mrs. Gay came to give her decision in respect to the comparative value which was to be assigned to the performances of John and Benny, the judgment was — to the surprise of both the boys — that the value of John's work in a given time was not only twice, but *four times* as great as that of Benny's. The way in which she was led to give such a decision was this.

In reflecting on the subject, her first thought was, that, as John might be considered, in a general view of the subject, to be twice as large and strong as Benny, his work ought to be expected to be twice as great. This was her theory. But looking at the subject practically, she knew that this could not be right.

" Suppose," she said to herself, " I should have my choice of such a boy as John to

work for me for one hour in my garden, or
for Benny to work two-hours. I should of
course very much prefer John. John might
accomplish a great deal of real service in
an hour — while all that Benny would do
in *two* hours would be of very little value
indeed. And yet Benny is as smart a boy
of his age as John is, and as healthy and
strong; and he is moreover considerably
more than half as old as John."

So Mrs. Gay was puzzled. People are
very often puzzled in this way by apparent discrepancies which appear between
the conclusions they come to through theo-
retical reasonings, and those forced upon
them by the observation of facts. Mrs.
Gay was quite at a loss to know how to
decide the question, and her brother Edward, John's uncle, the young gentleman
who has already been spoken of in these
volumes, happening to come in that same
evening, to make a call, she determined to
ask him about it.

So she stated the question to him. Her
question was, however, a different one from
that which the children had proposed to
her. They only wished to know what the

proportion was between the value of John's work for a given time, and Benny's. She not only desired to know this, but also to understand how it happened that, since boys from the time they are old enough to walk and talk grow in strength and capacity very regularly, and since John, setting aside the mere years of babyhood, might be considered as about twice as old as Benny, he should be so much more than twice as capable as he, — as she felt confident that he was.

" Ah," said Edward, as soon as she had stated her difficulty to him, " it is a case of duplicate ratio."

Edward said this with rather an arch look, as if he intended to mystify his sister with his learned language.

"Ah, Edward!" said Mrs. Gay, " now you are going to talk mathematics."

" Well, then," said Edward, " if you don't like mathematics, I will talk common English, and say double rate. Duplicate ratio means double rate, and what I mean is that a boy, in growing older, increases his capacity at a double rate, — one by the increase of his strength, and the other by the increase of his knowledge.

" It is something as it is with a carpet,"
continued Edward. " You would like to
have me explain it by a carpet, rather than
by mathematics."

" Yes," said Mrs. Gay, with a smile, —
" a great deal."

" Well, then," said Edward, " if you
have one room twice as large as another
every way, it will take *four* times as much
carpeting to cover the floor, instead of
twice as much ; for when the floor doubles
its dimensions, it increases the surface at *a
double rate*, once for the length and once
for the breadth, and that will make the
carpet four times as large."

" That is curious," said John, who had
been listening to this conversation.

" Yes," said Edward ; " if one room had
been only twice as *long* as the other, and
had remained just as wide, then it would
have taken *twice* as much carpeting. And
if it had been twice as wide, and had remained just as long, *then* it would have
taken twice as much too. But being both
twice as long and twice as wide, it increases
at a double rate, — that is, it becomes four
times as large.

"So it is with John," continued Edward. "In growing older he grows both in strength and in knowledge. If he remained of the same size and strength exactly, and only doubled his knowledge and skill, he would double his capacity in that way alone. And so, if, when he was older, he *knew* no more, but had only doubled his *strength* by his growing, then he would have doubled his capacity in that way.

"But as he grows in both ways, and has doubled his strength and also his knowledge, he has increased his capacity at a double rate, or, as the mathematicians say, in a duplicate ratio, — but you don't like that phrase."

"I don't see why double rate is not just as good," said Mrs. Gay; "and it is certainly easier to understand."

"It is just as good for some purposes," said Edward. "And I admit it is much better for such a talk as this. And, John, you had better remember what I have told you about this, for when you come to study mathematics, you will have to deal with all sorts of rates of increase and decrease. Some kinds of things increase at a *triple* rate, or in a triplicate ratio."

" What kind of things ? " asked John.

" Why a trunk, for example. If you had a trunk of a certain size, and it should grow larger, and yet keep all the time of the same shape, it would increase the capacity of the interior at a triple rate, — once for the length, once for the breadth, and once for the thickness. That would make it eight times as capacious."

" No," said John, — " six times. Three times two are six."

" It seems as if it would be six times," said Edward, " but it is really eight, and I can prove it to you.

" Suppose you had a bundle just big enough to fill the trunk. Now suppose you double the trunk in length alone, leav- ing the breadth and height the same, you see it would now hold two bundles of that size."

John admitted that it would.

" Now suppose you double the breadth, so as to make the trunk twice as *wide* as well as twice as long, how many bundles will it hold then ? "

" Four," said John.

" And now," continued Edward, " if we

double the *height,* we shall have room for two tiers, one below and one above, and four bundles in each tier, which will make eight. The trunk will hold eight times as much."

Edward observed that by this time his auditors seemed to be becoming a little tired of these mathematical explanations, and so said no more on the general subject, but only added, —

" I think that a boy in growing older, from the time when he is two or three years old, increases his capacity for useful work in a duplicate ratio at least, and I don't know but he does more rapidly still. I am sure it is at least a double rate, and consequently that four hours of Benny's work would not more than equal one of John's."

Mrs. Gay was satisfied that this opinion was correct, and she gave her decision accordingly.

But John, who always wished to be generous with Benny, and not merely just, said that he would not ask him to pay four hours' work for one. He should be satisfied with two hours. This pleased Benny very much, and so it was arranged that John was to pay Benny one dollar an hour in greenbacks for all the work that Benny did for him, and that Benny was to pay John two dollars an hour for all that he did for Benny.

CHAPTER V.

SMALL CHANGE.

THE boys' greenbacks were found in practice to work extremely well. As soon as they were perfectly dry, they were put in circulation, and they answered the purposes of a currency to keep the reckoning and settle transactions between John and Benny very nicely. Benny worked at raking up weeds in the garden, and in various other ways, to help John, and John paid him for his work at the rate of a dollar an hour. Then John, when he worked for Benny, kept an account of the time that he was employed, and when it came up to an hour, Benny paid him two dollars.

One of the principal things which Benny wished John to do was to make boats for him. John made very nice boats of boards, some thin and some thick, according to the size that Benny required. The way he made them was this.

After selecting the piece of wood, he would plane it to the right width, taking care to narrow it somewhat at the end intended for the stern. Then he would screw up the board in the vice, and with a shave round off the corners of it at the other end, so as to form the bows. Then he would make masts, and bore holes in the board to insert them; and sometimes he furnished the masts with shrouds and other simple rigging, provided Benny had money enough to pay for so much work. When Benny found that his cash was getting low, he was generally very desirous that John should find him something to do, so that he could earn more.

Before long, however, the boys began to feel some inconvenience from the want of small change, — the greenbacks of course not representing anything less than a dollar. Accordingly, when Benny worked only half an hour, there was no way to pay him. The only way was to remember the time that he had worked, or perhaps mark it down somewhere with a piece of chalk, and then pay him some other day, when he had made up the hour.

Sometimes, moreover, Benny, after having commenced a job, would get tired by the time he had worked only a quarter of an hour, and would go away to play.

To meet this difficulty, John determined to make some small money. He could not make many different kinds, and so undertook at first only quarters. To make them, he first marked out upon a long thin and narrow strip of wood a number of circles, of about the size of a quarter of a dollar, and then carefully cut them out with a chisel.

He marked out the circles of course with his compasses, and after he had cut out the pieces as near to the line as he could with the chisel, — being however very careful not to touch the line itself, — he then trimmed them round more closely still with his knife, and finally smoothed and finished them with sand-paper.

To do this, he laid a sheet of sand-paper down upon a smooth board, and then, putting four or five of his round pieces together, side by side, he rubbed the edges of all together on the sand-paper, — giving them at the same time, at every stroke, a

sort of rolling motion, which rounded them
over very nicely indeed. When he had gone
all around the rims in this manner, he
found, on taking his pieces apart, that they
were almost as round and smooth as if
they had been turned in a lathe.

After John had thus shaped and finished
these little disks of wood, he oiled them,
and set them in the sun to dry.

He tried to think of some way of im-
pressing a stamp upon them, to make them
look more like pieces of money; but he
could not contrive any way, and so he gave
up that plan.

"And now," said Benny, " I want to get
one of the quarters as soon as I can. Give
me something to do that will take me a
quarter of an hour."

" Well," said John, " you may clear out
all the shavings from under my bench, and
carry them away and put them in the kind-
ling-box, and I will give you half a dollar."

" But you have not got any half dollars,"
said Benny.

" Oh, I will pay you with two of these
quarters," said John. " That is the same
thing."

"Oh, yes," said Benny.

When John's workshop was in use, he was accustomed, on closing his work for any day, to sweep the shavings under the bench, as carpenters and joiners usually do.

Then, when at last the stock of shavings increased so much as to begin to be inconvenient, John — and sometimes Benny — used to gather them all up and carry them by means of a basket into the house, and put them in a box near the kitchen-door, where Bridget used to keep the kindling-wood for her morning fire.

So Benny went to work and pulled out the shavings from under the bench, and began to pack them into the basket.

"Remember the rule," said John.

"What rule?" asked Benny.

"The rule about spilling any by the way," replied John. "If you scatter the shavings on the way, then you will have to get the broom and sweep the passages all over, to sweep them up. If you don't spill any by the way, then you will save all that trouble, and so you will earn your quarter so much easier."

Benny was careful, on hearing this, to

4

crowd the shavings down well into the basket, and when he was ready to carry them
away, he examined the sides of the basket,
and the edges, to see if there were any
shavings ready to fall out.

He carried rather more than half the
shavings in the first load, so that by going
twice he had the work done. It did not
take more than fifteen minutes to finish the
job, and then Benny received his two quarters. He could not take them away with
him, it is true, for they were not yet dry, —
but John set them aside for him by pushing them to a separate part of the board,
and Benny, considering them as thus trans-
ferred to his possession, looked upon them
as his own, and began capering about with
delight. " I earned that half dollar pretty
quick, did not I ? " said he.

"Yes," said John; " you worked by the
job then, and the job turned out to be
quite a profitable one."

" How do you mean ? " asked Benny.

"Why, you did not work by time," said
John; " that is, I did not agree to pay you
according to the time it took, but to pay
you so much for doing the work, whether

the time it took was longer or shorter. I don't think it took you more than a quarter of an hour, and you earned *two* quarters of a dollar instead of *one*, as you would have done if you had been working by the hour. So you see you had a profitable job."

" I mean to work always by the job," said Benny.

" We will see," said John.

" But now, John," said Benny, " I want you to make me another vessel. I have got two, and I want three, so as to have a fleet. Uncle Edward says there can't be less than three for a fleet."

" Well," said John, " I will make you one for a quarter of a dollar."

Benny looked at his two quarters which were still lying in their place upon the board, but did not like the idea of parting with either of them.

"Ah, John," said he, " that is too much."

" Then I will do it by time," said John. " I will make it as quick as I can, and reckon the time, and then you shall pay me at the rate of two dollars an hour."

Benny hesitated a moment, and then he

said, " No, you may make the boat, and I
will give you a quarter of a dollar for it."

So John proceeded to make another
boat. It was quite a small one, for the
pond was altogether too small for large
vessels. I don't think this last vessel was
more than three inches long.

When it was finished, — with masts,
bowsprit, and all, complete, — Benny pushed back one of his quarters toward those
that still belonged to John, and then they
both went out to the pond to sail the new
vessel.

Benny put this boat in, with the other
two, and after pushing them all about a
few minutes, while John sat near, on the
edge of the platform, looking on, he stopped
and said, with an air of extreme dissatis-
faction,—

" John, this pond is a great deal too little.
Only just three vessels are enough to fill it
up so that they can't sail at all."

" I wish you had a larger one," said
John.

" Could you make a bigger one ? " asked
Benny.

" How big ? " rejoined John.

THE PUMP PLATFORM. *Page 52.*

Here Benny turned round and walked off, taking three long strides, as long as his little legs were capable of measuring.

Then stopping and turning round again, and planting his heel upon the ground to mark the spot, he said, — " So big."

" Perhaps I could," said John. " But then," he added, shaking his head and looking very grave, " it would cost a great deal of money."

" How much ? " asked Benny, still remaining where he was and inclining his head a little to one side, the better to hear the answer — which, moreover, he seemed to await with some anxiety.

John paused and seemed to be making a computation. At length he announced the conclusion that he had come to, by saying, —

" Twenty dollars."

Benny's countenance fell. For him to attempt to earn and accumulate twenty dollars seemed to him a very great undertaking. It is no wonder that he felt discouraged.

" We might, I suppose," said John, " make it in partnership, perhaps, and so

own it together. In that case you would
only have ten dollars to pay."

This suggestion afforded a sensible re-
lief to Benny's anxiety, and he responded
in a tone of great satisfaction, —

"Well, I should like that."

"And perhaps," said John, "you might
do some of the work yourself, by helping
me make it."

"Yes," said Benny, "I am sure I could."

"I will talk with uncle Edward about
it," said John, "the first time I see him."

"Or Ebenezer," said Benny.

"No," replied John, "not Ebenezer. He
would not take any interest in a pond to
sail little boats in."

•

CHAPTER VI.

A CONFERENCE.

John and Benny took an early opportunity to consult their uncle Edward about their proposed pond. It was one evening when he had called in to make a little visit, and he was sitting with them upon the piazza.

John told him that Benny wanted a larger place to sail his boats in.

" He has got nothing now," said John, " but a little spout, under the pump, and he wants a good big pond. Do you think there is any way that I could make one ? "

" Such things have been done," said Edward, assuming a very grave and business-like air. " I have known of several cases, of making quite large ponds."

" How did they do it ? " asked John.

" The first one that I ever heard of," said Edward, " was made a long time ago. The way they did was to find a low place near some running water, and then dig the ground out."

" Was it near a brook ? " asked Benny.

" A brook or else a river," said Edward. " It was a stream of running water. That is a very good way to make a pond, if you can find a low level place near a brook on your grounds."

" We have not got any brook," said John.

" Perhaps we might make a brook," suggested Benny.

" Oh, no," replied John, impatiently. " You cannot make a brook."

" Why, yes," said Benny, " we might dig a little place along the ground, and then when the rain comes the water would run there, and that would make a brook."

" Oh, that would not be anything but a *rain*-brook," said John. " That would not do any good."

" All brooks are rain-brooks," said Edward.

" Oh, no," replied John. " I know brooks that run all the time, whether it rains or not. They run in the pleasant weather."

" Yes," said Edward; " but that is because

the water from the last rains has not yet all drained off out the ground. They run slower and slower in pleasant weather, and if the pleasant weather should continue long enough, the brook would get entirely dry.

"So would the rivers too," continued Edward. "They all come from the water of the rain, draining slowly out of the ground, in little brooks, and finally in rivers, when the brooks come together and make rivers. But if it should stop raining for some years, all the water would be drained off, and the brooks and rivers would all dry up."

John and Benny paused a moment, thinking of the state of things which such a change, if it were really to take place, would introduce, and then John said, —

"At any rate, we could not make a brook that would do us any good."

"No," said Edward; "if you were going to make a pond in that way, you would have to find a natural brook. And then it would be a very muddy piece of work digging it, for the ground in such places is wet. Besides, it would take an enormous

while to make it, — that is, if you make it
as large as the one I am speaking of."

" How large was that ? " asked John.

" The people that saw it at the time it
was made," replied Edward, " said it was
four hundred and fifty miles round, and
three hundred feet deep. The name of it
was Lake Moeris."

Edward said this in a perfectly grave
and serious manner, just as if he did not
know that it was entirely impossible for
the boys to make such an immense reser-
voir as this."

"Hoh! uncle Edward," said John; " we
could not make such a big pond as that."

" I don't think that Lake Moeris was
really as big as that, after all," said Edward.   " They said it was, at the time ; but
that was two thousand years ago, and they
used to tell pretty large stories in those days.
The lake is there now, and people sometimes go to see it. It is not now more
than one hundred miles round instead of
four hundred and fifty. Perhaps it has got
filled up a good deal in the course of two
thousand years, — or perhaps they told too
big stories about it."

"*I* believe they told big stories about it," said John. "They never could dig out a pond four hundred and fifty miles round."

"At any rate, it was a great deal too big for what you want. So I will tell you about some smaller ones."

Edward then proceeded to describe the docks that have been excavated for shipping in London and Liverpool. These, like Lake Moeris, were excavated in comparatively low places, near a river, so that the water of the river could flow into them at high tide and fill them. The walls of them were built, Edward said, of solid masonry, and there was a broad quay, and ranges of great stores and warehouses around them, so that they looked like open squares of water in the heart of a great city.

"If you could build a dock like one of these," said Edward, "by digging out a large square hole in some low and swampy ground near a brook, and then build walls of brick all along the sides to keep the sides from caving in, and then make a good hard roadway around the margin, and finally build a row of stores and warehouses

outside of the road, to keep your cargoes
in, and stand under while it rains, it would
be just what you want."

The boys listened very attentively while
Edward said this, wholly absorbed in the
idea of such a charming place for their
boats and their navigation as he had pict-
ured to their minds. They looked him
steadily in the face as he spoke, but they
did not perceive the slightest appearance
of any lurking smile upon his countenance.

John was satisfied that Edward entirely
overrated his powers as a mechanic, in im-
agining that he and Benny could construct
such a work as he described. But he felt
complimented by his uncle's even conceiv-
ing of the possibility of it.

" We never could do it in the world,"
said John, shaking his head disconsolately.

" Besides," said Benny, " we should get
all muddy."

" There are some places," said Edward,
" where you can dig out a place for a pond
without having any muddy work at all to
do. I knew of a fellow once, — I don't
know that I ought to call him a fellow
though, for he was a man, although he was
not a very large one."

" What was his name ? " asked John.

" Louis," said Edward. " At least, that was his first name. He wanted a place for his vessels, and so he set some workmen to make one for him, on the part of the ground where it was not wet at all. In fact it was all rocks there. So the men went to work drilling holes everywhere in the rocks, and putting in charges of gunpowder to blast them out. It took them a good many years; but at last they got it done. They filled it by letting in water from the sea."

" I should like to see it," said John.

" Very likely you may see it some day," replied Edward. " It is at a place called Cherbourg, on the coast of France. I advise you to look it out on your map tomorrow, and see how you get to it from Paris, and how far it is. If you ever go to Europe, you will certainly go to Paris, and then, if it is not too far, you can go to Cherbourg and see this great basin. And you may see Napoleon, the man that had it made."

" Napoleon ? " said John ; " you said his name was Louis."

" Yes," rejoined Edward, " Louis Napoleon."

" But, uncle Edward," said Benny, after a pause, " *we* can't make our pond in any such ways as that. We can't blast out the rocks, and then, besides, there is no sea, nor river, nor brook, nor anything, to fill it with."

" Except a pump," said Edward, quietly.

" Yes," said John, " we have got a pump."

" Sometimes," said Edward, " people make reservoirs and ponds far away from any brook or river, in quite dry places where it is easy digging. There is a great pond made in this way in the Park in New York. I saw them when they were digging it. You could walk about all over the bottom of it."

" That will be the best kind for us to make," said John.

" Yes," replied Edward, " only when a pond is made on high and dry ground, you have a good deal to do to make the bottom and the walls tight, so that the water will not all leak away."

" How do you do it ? " asked John.

"They generally line the bottom and walls with what they call *concrete*," said Edward, "and that is a mixture of gravel and small stones with a kind of mortar that will grow hard under water."

"I don't think we could make anything like that," said John, shaking his head.

"No," replied Edward, "not unless you had plenty of hydraulic cement, which is what they make the mortar of. It is a sort of dark-colored powder, and comes in barrels."

"Will it go off?" asked Benny.

"Oh, no," said Edward, "it is not that kind of powder. It looks like flour, only it is of a dark color. It costs two or three dollars a barrel."

"We could not get any of it," said John, despondingly..

"You might make the walls and bottom of your pond tight in some other way, perhaps," said Edward. "Perhaps you might make them of boards — provided you could fit them together pretty well.

"If you could only make a large shallow box," continued Edward, his countenance suddenly brightening up as if at last

a promising idea had struck him, — " as
large as you want your pond to be, and
with sides as high as you want your pond
to be deep, and caulk the cracks with rags,
or fill them up with clay, and bank up all
around the box with sand to make a
pretty shore, and then fill it with water
from the pump, I don't know but that you
might make a very good pond."

The truth is that John's uncle, Edward,
had exactly this plan in his mind from the
beginning. But he came to it gradually,
and in this roundabout way, partly for the
sake of amusing the children by his talk,
and partly to instruct them; — for when
he found that they were particularly interested in any subject about their play, he
used always in talking with them in relation to it, to contrive to connect with it as
much instruction as he could.

After some further conversation, the boys
fully determined on trying to make a pond
on the plan which Edward had proposed.
Edward said that if they would proceed
slowly and carefully with the work, and not
attempt to get it done in a hurry, and
would promise always to stop at once

when they came to any serious difficulty and wait till he came to tell them what to do, — then he would undertake the general superintendence of the work, and would come every day or two and see how they got along.

There was a pile of old fence-boards in a corner behind one of the sheds, which Edward recollected, and which he said would answer very well for making the box, if Mrs. Gay would give John permission to use them. John went in to ask her, and she said yes, without any hesitation.

So Edward gave John and Benny directions as to what they were to do the first day in beginning their work, and the conference on the subject of the pond ended.

5

CHAPTER VII.

WORKING SYSTEMATICALLY.

The boys began their work the very next day. The first thing was to go out to the pile of boards in order to select such as would be suitable for their purpose.

Many boys in such a case as this would have tumbled the pile of boards all over and left them in confusion, and would moreover have split and spoiled many good boards in trying to pull them out from under the pile, without first carefully taking off those that were above them. But John had learned more wisdom than this by seeing how Ebenezer was accustomed to handle boards.

" Now, Benny," said he, " you go to one end of the boards and I will go to the other, and we will take them up one by one. As fast as we come to good ones we will lay them over by themselves, back a little way, and those we do not want we will lay down close to the pile, so that we can easily put them where they belong again, when we have taken out all that we want."

Benny succeeded in lifting his end of each board very well; and by pursuing the method which John had indicated, the two boys had soon selected enough for their purpose. The rest they put back carefully in their places on the pile again.

· " Now," said John, " we must carry these boards that we have taken out, round to the shed, and sweep them all on both sides with a good stiff broom."

" What is that for ? " asked Benny. " They don't look very dirty."

" No," replied John, " but Ebenezer says that boards that have been laying out in this way get a great deal of sand and dust upon them that dulls the saws when we try to saw them, unless we brush them very clean."

The boys accordingly carried the boards around to the shed, and there swept them all off thoroughly, both sides and edges, with the broom.

John then, with Benny's help, took up the shortest of the boards, intending to see how

long a piece he could get out of that, in
order to make that the measure of the others.   He marked off a line as near one end
as it would go and avoid the roughness
and the cracks, taking care to make the
line square with one of the sides of the
board, and then sawed the end off.   Then
he measured with the long arm of his
square as far as he could go safely, toward
the other end.   He found that he could get
ten feet very easily.   So they determined
to have the pond ten feet long.   This
pleased Benny very much, as he found that
it would make the pond considerably larger
than he had indicated by his pacing, at the
pump.

John proceeded in this way to measure
off and saw the other boards until he cal-
culated that he had enough, all of the same
length, to make the bottom and sides of
his box.   He selected two of the same
width, for the sides, and laid them aside,
reserving the rest to make the bottom.

"And now, Benny," said he, " we must
decide how wide we will have it."

" Let us have it as wide," said Benny,
" as we possibly can."

" We will lay down the bottom-boards on the floor, side by side," said John, " and see how wide a bottom they will make."

So John sawed out the two end-boards, making them seven feet long. When these were ready, the boys piled up the whole together neatly, where they would be safe and out of the way, and then went out to play.

They told Edward, that evening, how much they had done. He said they were very wise in not attempting to do any more the first day.

" The chief reason," said he, " why boys fail in so many things that they undertake is, that they are always in so desperate a hurry to get their work done."

" We thought we would stop," said John, " as soon as we had got the stuff cut out, and not begin to nail it together until to-morrow."

" But nailing it together is not the next thing," said Edward. " The next thing is to bore the holes. Never nail without boring. Is not that one of Ebenezer's rules ? "

" Yes," said John ; " but it won't take us long to bore the holes. We can bore them as we nail them."

" No," said Edward ; " bore all the holes before you nail a single one. That is the best way, or else you won't do them systematically and scientifically. How many holes do you think you will have to bore ? "

" Oh, there will be a good many," said John, " I suppose. There will be a dozen or two."

" How many bottom-boards have you got ? " asked Edward.

" Seven," replied John.

" There must be three holes in each end of each bottom-board," said Edward, " one in the middle and one near each edge. That makes six for each board, and seven times six is forty-two. Then there must be one every foot along the lower edge of each side-board. How long are the side-boards ? "

" Ten feet," said John.

" That will take twenty more holes." said Edward, " and that makes sixty-two. Then there will be three at each end of the end-boards, where they are nailed to the ends of the side-boards. That will make six more, — sixty-eight. Then you ought to have two stiffening pieces to go along under the bottom."

" What for ? " asked John.

" Why, you see," said Edward, " that the bottom-boards being long, and only nailed at the two ends, will be likely to spring in the middle if there comes any unequal pressure or strain upon them, and that will open the seams. So you ought to have two cleats, that is narrow boards, to nail across the bottom, about two feet from the two ends. That will make your box a great deal stronger and tighter."

" I have not got out any boards for that," said John.

" You can cut some out then," said Edward. " They must be as long as your box is wide, and about four inches wide. These cleats must be nailed to the bottom-boards, two nails to each board; that will make, — let me see, seven boards and two nails for each cleat and each board, — that makes twenty-eight more. These, added to the sixty-eight we had before, make ninety-six, — almost a hundred holes to be bored, you see."

" Oh, dear me ! " said John; " we never can bore so many holes as that."

" Then you had better give up making

your pond," said Edward, "and carry the
boards back to-morrow and put them on
the pile again."

John shook his head.

" I advise you to take two days for the
boring of these holes," said Edward, "and
to do it thoroughly and well. The boards
are about an inch thick, I suppose, and as
you want the nails to go in at the middle
of the thickness, the holes must come half
an inch from the ends of the boards to be
nailed. You had better measure the half
inch, and draw a line so as to get your
nail-holes exactly in the range, and be careful to bore them through straight."

John and Benny concluded, on the whole,
to follow Edward's advice, and take two
days for boring the hundred holes, though
finally Edward told them that they had better not bore the holes in the cleats until they
were ready to be put on, as they could not
tell, in respect to them, exactly where the
nails would come. All the rest would come
exactly half an inch from the end or edge of
the board that was to be nailed. So that
if they took two days for the boring, they
would have about forty holes to bore each
day.

Accordingly, the next day when the time arrived for going to their work, John selected a gimlet of the proper size, — that is, one a little smaller than the nails were that he had decided to use, — and began. He took one board at a time, and with Benny's help he laid it across his two benches, — for before this time he had made two benches to saw upon. He had first however placed the benches at such a distance apart that the board would extend an inch or two each way beyond them, in order that he might bore his holes near the ends, without boring into the benches.

Next he marked lines half an inch from each end of the board, and then proceeded to bore the holes, one in the middle and one near each corner, taking great care to bore them straight. Benny stood by to help him, and he did help him a great deal, by handing him the tools as he wanted them, and taking them away when he was done with them. After one board was bored, they laid it carefully away, and then took another, and so they worked on quietly and steadily for an hour, at the end of which time they found that half the boring was done.

" Now," said John, " we will put the work away for to-day."

" Why, I am not tired," said Benny.

" Neither am I," said John ; " but uncle Edward said, that, if we meant to make a good job of it, we must always leave off our work *before* we *began* to get tired."

This was excellent advice ; for the work of this kind that boys do after they begin to get tired is almost always badly done.

The next day John and Benny finished the boring of all the boards, and John went into the town and bought two pounds of nails, which, as nearly as he could estimate, would be enough for the whole job. He brought the nails home, and opening the paper he poured them out into an open nail-box that he had provided for that purpose. He also put the hammer in the box upon the top of the nails, and then put the box upon the pile of boards which he had been preparing.

" There, Benny," said he, " now we are all ready. To-morrow we will begin upon the nailing."

CHAPTER VIII.

THE POND-BOX.

THE plan which John was disposed to adopt in respect to the making and the subsequent ownership of the pond, was to keep an account of the number of hours which he and Benny worked upon it, and then for them to own it at the end in shares, in proportion to the value of the labor which each had expended upon it, estimating his work as worth twice as much as Benny's, for the same time.

By this plan it is plain that no money would be required in the transaction. The whole business would be a matter of account.

But Benny did not quite like this plan. The money was all made, and he did not see why it might not be used. He wanted to be paid a dollar an hour for all the work he did.

" Very well," said John ; " I can pay you

as you go along for all you do upon the box, and then the pond will be all mine when it is done."

" And can't I sail my boats on it at all ? " said Benny.

" Oh, yes," replied John ; " I should let you sail your boats on it, I suppose ; but it would be my pond."

" But it ought to be part mine," said Benny, " because I help you make it. I work on it always when you do."

" Yes," said John; " but then if I pay you for what you do, then it becomes my work."

" No," said Benny, " it is not your work. It is my work. And my work is harder than yours, for I have to lift such heavy boards."

John could not help smiling to perceive that Benny could not understand so simple an idea, as that whoever paid for the work was entitled to the avails of it. So he very wisely determined to give up the attempt, and let Benny learn gradually by the progress of the work, and by the experience that he would acquire, how the case really stood. This was a very wise

conclusion, for learning by practical experience is after all the best way to become
acquainted with the nature of any com-
plicated system, such as the management
of joint-stock companies like this that
John and Benny were engaged in.

John therefore, as all older brothers ought
to do in such cases, concluded at once to
fall in with Benny's ideas, and yield to his
wishes, — knowing very well that he could
make it all right in the end. So he went
on regularly paying him a dollar an hour
for every hour that he worked upon the
" pond-box," as he called it.

As soon as the holes were bored and the
box was ready to be nailed together, the
question at once arose in respect to the
precise spot where it should be placed. It
was evident that it must be near the pump,
inasmuch as it was from that source that
it was to be supplied with water. There
were some difficulties, however, for the
ground was a little sloping there, and John
knew very well that the pond must be
level. Then, besides, that part of the yard
was very smooth and green, and John was
not quite sure that his mother would be

willing to have the pond there. So he
brought her out to see.

When his mother was upon the ground,
John explained the plan to her, and told
her what progress they had made. The
box, he said, was all ready to be nailed together. Mrs. Gay had heard the boys
talking about the plan, and knew that they
were at work upon something of the kind,
but she did not think that they would really accomplish anything, and so she paid
little attention to the subject, — except to
feel pleased that they had something to
occupy their spirit of industry, and make
them happy. But now when John brought
her out upon the ground and said that the
box was ready to be put together, and explained how large it was to be, and proposed to place it on the greensward of the
yard a little way from the pump, the business began to assume quite a serious as-
pect.

" You will have to dig off the turf, I
suppose," said his mother, " in order to
make the ground level."

"Yes, mother," said John, " we can do
that, or else we can wheel on some earth

in our wheelbarrow, and level up the low part."

" Then we are going to bank up all around our pond with sand, to make a pretty shore," said Benny.

It is very plain that the placing of the pond, as the children proposed, would seriously deface the yard, and make quite a litter there, to be cleared away whenever the works should be abandoned.

Mrs. Gay however said nothing. She looked at the ground, asked more questions, and then said, —

" Very well. Now I understand the plan. I think it is a very good idea for you to make such a pond, but as for the place I must take a little time to consider. I will tell you what conclusion I come to, this afternoon. You can't do any work upon your box this morning, for it is nearly time now for John to go to school."

The boys were satisfied with this, for their mother seldom gave an answer in any very important cases like this without " taking time to consider."

After John had gone to school, Mrs. Gay came out to look at the ground again.

She saw very clearly that the digging and filling-in which would be necessary in setting the pond-box in its place would greatly deface the yard, and make a very ugly place after it was cleared away, however carefully and nicely Wilmot might smooth it over. It would leave, she thought, a sort of *scar* upon the ground, which would not disappear all summer.

Still, although Mrs. Gay was very nice and particular about her garden and grounds, she set a far higher value upon the improvement and happiness of her children than upon any of the charms of verdure and rural beauty about her residence. She would not allow the children to deface or destroy anything, or make disorder anywhere, wantonly, and from mere momentary caprice; but she was always ready to appropriate any part of her premises — that is of her house and grounds — to their pleasure or profit, whenever the advantage to be gained made it seriously worth while.

"In this case," said she to herself, "I think it *is* worth while. If they can really make a pond as large as they say, they will

amuse themselves at it a great deal; and
when they have done with it, Wilmot can
clear everything away in a few hours; and
then the place will be just the same as it
was before, except that it will take a little
time for the grass to grow.

While Mrs. Gay was thinking these
things, sauntering slowly about the place,
she happened to turn round the corner of
the building, and there she came accidentally upon a spot which she thought at once
would make a much more convenient and
suitable location for the pond than the one
which the children had chosen. It was a
small vacant spot near the end of a building, with pretty copses of shrubbery on
each side, and an open space in the centre.
The pump was out of sight from the
place, being hidden partly by the building
and partly by the great lilac-bush which is
seen in the picture of the pump in a pre-
ceding engraving.

Still Mrs. Gay perceived that there was
room behind the lilac-bush for the spout,
or aqueduct, by which John was to convey
the water from the pump to the pond; and
the distance to the place where the nearest

corner of the pond would come was not great.

Mrs. Gay observed too, — and this was a very important point, — that the ground at this new locality was enough lower than the platform of the pond to cause the wa- ter to run freely in the aqueduct when it was made. The ground too was soft there, and comparatively free from grass, being somewhat shaded by the shrubbery; so that it would be much easier, Mrs. Gay thought, for the boys to make a proper excavation there to set the pond-box in.

Accordingly, when John came home after school, she took him out and showed him the new place. She was willing, she said, that he should have the place which he had first chosen, unless he should think that this place would be better. But when she ex- plained to him the advantages of the new place, both he and Benny thought that it would be a great deal better.

" We can make a seat *there*, Benny," said John, pointing, — " next to the house, and we can sit upon it to see our boats sail."

Accordingly, when the time came for resuming their work that afternoon, they brought the boards out, one by one, to the ground, and began to nail the box together. They were of course obliged to make the box bottom upwards, for the bottom-boards could in no other way be nailed to the side and end-boards. Benny held one of the end-boards up edgewise on the ground, while John nailed the end of one of the bottom-boards to it, leaving the other end to rest upon the ground.

When one end had been nailed, he went to the other end and raised that from the ground, and put the other end-board under it and nailed that too. He proceeded in this way nailing on board after board until all the bottom-boards were in their places. The nailing, now that the holes were bored, was very easy and rapid work, especially as Benny stood by all the time ready to help John put the boards in their place, and to keep them steady until the nails took hold, and also to hand him the nails as fast as he wanted them.

When the bottom-boards were nailed to the end-pieces, John fitted the side-pieces on, in their places, and nailed them, and finally nailed the two cleats upon the bottom, as Edward had recommended, and the box was done, — only it was bottom upwards.

" Now," said John, " here is a trouble which I did not think of. How are we ever going to get such a monstrous big box turned over? *We* can't lift it — you and I."

" We must get uncle Edward to help us," said Benny.

" Yes," replied John ; " he said he would help us if we got into any difficulty. But first we must get the place ready."

The plan which Edward had recommended was that the pond-box should be set a few inches at least into the ground, as he said that would help prevent the water from leaking out of it so fast. So John brought some tools, and he and Benny prepared to dig away the ground from the space where the box was to be placed.

The back line of this excavation they made about three feet from the building, so as to leave room for a seat, and also for a walk in front of it. John, who had by this time begun to acquire quite a taste for measuring and marking, measured off the distances accurately, and put stakes down at the corners of the excavation to be made, and then stretched a twine from one stake to another all around, just as he had seen Wilmot mark out beds in the garden, with the garden-line.

Then he and Benny dug out the ground inside of this line, about four inches deep, as near as they could judge, and smoothed the bottom of it off, as level as they could. Just as they were finishing this work they heard a pleasant voice calling out, —

" Johnny ! Benny ! Where are you ?"

" There is cousin Mary," said John. " Run out and tell her where we are. " At the same time John called as loud as he could, — " Here we are ! Mary, come round here ! "

Mary soon appeared, Benny conducting her and showing her the way. She stood for a moment struck with surprise at seeing what a great work of construction the children were engaged in.

CHAPTER IX.

MARY'S HELP.

WHEN Mary came to understand what the boys were making, she was very much interested in the plan. Benny showed her one of the greenbacks too, and one of the quarters, which John had made, and told her that John paid him a dollar an hour for all the work he did in helping make the pond-box.

" I wish I had some money," said Mary.

" You must work then and earn some," said Benny.

" Well," said Mary, " I will.   But what can I do ? "

" I will tell you what she can do, Benny," said John.   " She can make you some sails for the vessels you are going to have on this pond.   You might give her a greenback dollar for every two sails that she would make for you.   Then I can put them on the masts of the vessels."

Mary said she would make the sails if John would give her a pattern. John said he would. He would cut out a pattern of the shape of the sail in paper, and then Mary must cut out the sails and make a broad hem on one side for the mast to go through, and another along the bottom for the boom.

"And when you get the money," said Benny, "you can pay John with it for something that he will do for you. Is n't there something that you would like to have him make for you with his tools?"

"Yes," said Mary; "I want him to make a trellis for my climbing rose."

"John," said Mary, "can you make a trellis with your tools?"

"Yes," said John; "I think I could make a trellis pretty well."

Mary was very much pleased with the idea of having a trellis, and she said she·would make the sails the very first thing, as soon as John gave her the patterns.

Mary then asked the boys when they were going to turn the box over. She longed to see it right side up.

"I do, too," said John, "but it is too heavy. We have got to wait till uncle Edward comes to help us."

"Oh, no," said Mary, "*we* can turn it over. At least you can lift up one side of it a little way, to see how heavy it is, and I will put a stick of wood under to keep it up."

The boys concluded to try this plan, and Mary went to bring a stick of wood. The boys took hold of the side of the box by insinuating their fingers under the edge of it, and then lifted. As soon as the edge came up a little from the ground, Mary slipped the stick of wood underneath, and that kept it up.

The boys stopped to rest.

"There," said Mary, "it is partly up. Now you can get hold better. You might lift it up higher now, if I only had something to put under."

John said he would go and get a board. So he went to his shop and presently returned with two boards, one about a foot long, and the other two or three feet.

"Now," said Mary, "lift again, and I will set this short board under."

So John and Benny lifted again, and Mary put the board under, by way of prop, to keep it up. It did keep it up, but the box did not rest upon it very steadily. There seemed to be a tendency in the board to fall over to one side or the other and let the box down again.

" Now," said Mary, " lift again, and I will put the long board under. We shall get it all the way up by and by."

" No," said John. " I am afraid if we get it up much higher it might fall down on us and break our legs. I wish we had somebody to help us. Bridget might come. Benny, go in and ask Bridget if she would be willing to come out here and help us lift up a box."

Benny ran round the corner of the house to the kitchen-door, to call Bridget, while John kept the box steady upon the board where they had poised it. Bridget soon came out to see what was to be done.

She comprehended the state of the case at a glance.

" Oh, yes," said she, " I will turn your mortar-bin over for you. Stand out of the way."

So saying, she advanced to the side of the box where John was standing, and putting herself in his place there, she seized hold of the edge of the box, and, knocking away the board with her foot, she lifted it up at once till she got it as high as her head, and then pushing still more, and yet holding it to prevent its going too far, she soon brought it into an upright position upon one of its sides.

" There," said she, " now go round to the other side and hold your long board up for a prop, while I let it down a little way to rest upon it."

So John held the board for a prop as Bridget directed, and Bridget pushed the box gently over until the bottom of it rested upon it. Then she went round herself to the back side, and took hold of the box again on that side.

" There, now, pull it away," said she.

So John pulled the prop away, and Bridget then, with great apparent ease, lowered the box down to the ground. Then, with a little pushing and prying, the boys brought it to its place, and it settled down snugly into its bed.

"Good!" exclaimed John.

"Good!" repeated Benny.

Bridget turned and began to walk away back toward her kitchen.

The boys called out to her as she went, saying, "Thank you, Bridget!"

"And now," said John, "how shall we know when the box is exactly level?"

"Set a basin of water in it," said Bridget, as she walked away round the corner.

"A basin of water!" repeated John; — then, after a moment's pause, he seemed suddenly to perceive how a basin of water would answer the purpose of a level, and so he sent Mary into the house to bring one.

When the basin came, John set it down carefully in the middle of the box. They saw on examining the surface of the water in the basin that it rose a little higher on one side than on the other, thus revealing the fact that one end of the box was somewhat higher than the other.

The children then all three got into the box, and stood upon the bottom of it near the end which seemed to be the highest, and then jumped about a little, and so soon settled that end until the water appeared level. Then they banked up the loose earth around the margin of the box, trampling it down hard, and the box was fixed securely in its place.

After this, John made a seat against the wall of the building on the back side of the box, and levelled and smoothed the ground in front of the seat, to make a path there, along the side of the box. He also opened a path along one end of it, to lead in toward the seat. The bushes and shrubbery came so near to the margin of the box on the other side, that there was no room to pass there.

When Edward came to see what the boys had done, he approved of it all fully. John said that he was going to make a watercourse, by nailing two narrow side-pieces upon a long and narrow board, so as to form a very long trough; and then, when he wanted to fill up his pond, he could lay down this trough in a slanting position, close under the lilac-bushes, with one end under the nose of the pump, and the other reaching over the corner of the box; and then he and Benny might pump water in at one end, and it would flow into the box from the other.

This would have been a very good plan, but Edward proposed a better one, which was to make a straight trough close under the margin of the piazza, from opposite the pump to the corner of the box, and to fasten it there permanently; and then to make a short conduit of the same kind to go from the nose of the pump, or rather from the end of the "shoe," to the nearest end of the long one. In this way the boys, when they had done filling their pond at any time, would only have to remove and take care of the short piece, which would be very easily managed, — the chief portion of the aqueduct being close under the edge of the piazza, where it was out of the way. You will understand this plan better by studying it out in the engraving.

Edward assisted John a good deal in respect to the work of making and placing the aqueduct, and the boys afterward wheeled a great many loads of sand, which they dug out of a bank, and this sand they spread all around the margin of the box.

They also shovelled a good deal of sand into the box, and spread it around there, and banked it up at the sides, so as to make a natural-looking bottom, and a gradually deepening shore.   Benny even heaped up a quantity of sand and several stones in one corner, nearly up to the level of where the water would come, in order to make a dangerous place, for his vessels to get wrecked in.

When all was ready, they began to pump the water, — all three, Mary, Benny, and John, taking turns at the work. While one was pumping, the other two ran round to see the water pouring in from the end of the aqueduct into the pond, and to observe how it spread over the sand, and gradually rose higher and higher. Benny could not wait for the pond to be full, but put his vessels in at once, — the three that he had, — placing them upon the sand; and had the pleasure of seeing them floated up one after another, by the rising of the tide. You will see a representation of this scene in the frontispiece.

John paid Benny regularly a dollar an hour for all the work that he did upon the pond. He also paid Mary, although he had not promised to do so. But she had really helped them a great deal, and he thought it only just and right that she should be paid.

Thus the pond was entirely his, when it was finished. But he did not say so to Benny, knowing that it would only trouble him to seem to be excluded from any share in the possession of it, and he knew it could do no harm to have Benny imagine that he owned a part of it too, notwithstanding that he had been fully paid for all the work that he had done upon it.

" It will make no difference," said he to himself. " I am willing that he should sail his boats in it as much as he likes, — provided he lets it remain where it is, — and he can't very well take it up and carry it away, under pretence that he is the owner of it."

CHAPTER X.

THE TRELLIS.

By the time that the pond was finished, John found himself pretty heavily in debt. He had paid to Benny five dollars and three quarters, for work which he had done, and Mary two dollars and one quarter for the help which she had rendered. This made seven dollars in all; and as the condition on which the greenbacks and the other money was issued was that John was to receive them all back again in payment for work which he would do for the holders of the money, he now saw that he was in fact seven dollars in debt, which he was to pay in work at two dollars an hour. In other words, he was bound to do three hours and a half work for Mary and Benny, whenever they called upon him for it, in order to redeem the currency which he had put in circulation.

Thus it seems that John's money, though

the material of which it was made was
wood, was of the nature of paper money,
which is always a promise to pay, by
somebody or other, — generally the bank
or government, — some substantial equiva-
lent for it when it is brought in.

It is true that bank-bills and real greenbacks, like John's imitations of them, look
very pretty, and many persons attach a certain value to them on their own account.
But they would soon lose all this value if
people did not believe that they would be
redeemed by something substantial when
they were brought in, to those who issued
them.

In the same manner Benny liked the
first greenback which he received, on its
own account, and John might for a time
have gone on making more, and paying
the children with them for the work they
did for him. But every one that he issued
in this way would only have increased the
number of hours' work for them which he
would have to do in the end, if he meant
faithfully to redeem them. And if he did
not mean to redeem them, but put the
children off with excuses when they came

7

with them to get him to do something for
them, then they would soon have ceased to
value them, and would not have been willing to work for them any more.

So John, in order to keep up the credit
of his currency, determined not to put out
any more money, if he could help it, but
to get back what he had already issued as
fast as he could, by working for it; and
thus he could issue it again.

So he went to work at once on Mary's
trellis. He first drew a plan of it under
Mary's direction, at his desk, at the window called the morning window, in the
sitting-room.

I think every boy ought to have a desk
or something of the kind, in some convenient place in the sitting-room, where it is
always warm and comfortable, and have
it provided with everything necessary for
writing, and drawing, and doing other such
work, — that is, I mean every boy that has
intelligence and manliness enough to take
care of such a place, and to keep it in order. He might call it his office. That
was the name that John gave to his corner
by the morning window. By having such

facilities for the execution of any literary work that he may have to do, a boy will often employ himself in this way, when, without them, he would do nothing of the kind. And by thus employing himself he will insensibly make great improvement, and acquire a facility in managing a pencil or a pen which will be of great service to him in his studies, and in his general progress at school.

When John began to talk with Mary about the trellis, the first thing he said was,

" Come to my office, and we will make a drawing of it."

So Mary went with John to his office, and there John took out a pencil and a ruler, and also his book of plans.

The ruler was a foot long, and it had the inches and tenth of inches marked upon it. John called it a scale.

" I don't see what you call it a scale for," said Benny, who was standing by. " You can't weigh anything with it."

" No," said John ; " it does not mean a scale for weighing. It comes from the Latin word, which means *ladder*."

" I don't think it is a ladder, either," said

Benny. " You can't climb up on anything by it."

" No," said John; " but don't you see all those little divisions along the edge ? They look something like the rounds of a long ladder.   That is the reason why they call it by a name that means ladder."

John asked Mary how large her trellis was to be.   She could not tell very well in feet and inches, but she reached her hand up as high as she could, and said she would like to have it as high as that, or higher.

" My climbing-rose," said she, " is already almost as high as my head, and I am sure it would grow a great deal higher if it had a good trellis.   It has not anything now but some old sticks, and the rose is so heavy upon them that they are all ready to tumble down."

After estimating as well as he could the dimensions that Mary indicated, John decided on making the trellis six feet high and four feet wide.   He would have it formed, he thought, of two upright pieces for the sides, and a number of cross-bars to be nailed across, — the bars to project a few inches beyond the uprights, on each side. He thought it would be sufficient to have the bars two inches wide and about six inches apart, and to have the lowest one two feet from the ground.

As the trellis was to be six feet high above the ground, and as the side-pieces ought to be driven down about one foot, that would require them to be seven feet long.

John made his drawing in accordance with these estimates. First he drew the forms of the side-pieces, arranging them up and down the page, and making them seven feet long and pointed at the lower ends, and about three inches wide. He placed them, too, three feet apart, from inside to inside.

Then he drew the cross-bars. He made them four feet long. Of course they projected three inches beyond the side-pieces. He placed the first cross-piece four inches below the top of the side-pieces, and the next one six inches below that, and the rest at the same distances from each other till he came within about three feet of the bottom of the side-pieces, which would make the lowest cross-piece come about two feet from the ground.

He made a little dot at each crossing of the cross-pieces and the side-pieces, to represent the nail by which they were to be nailed together.

John drew his plan on what he called the scale of half an inch to a foot, and he took so much pains to measure every part exactly, and to rule his lines neatly, that the drawing when it was done presented a very symmetrical and scientific appearance.

" What a pretty trellis it will be," said Mary, — " if you make it like that."

John began the work that day, and worked upon the job an hour, sawing out the strips. There was, of course, a great deal of sawing to be done, to get out so many pieces. John proceeded with the work, however, very scientifically, first selecting a smooth and straight - grained board, and sawing it to the length of the cross-pieces, — four feet, — and then dividing it by chalk - lines into the requisite number of parts, two inches wide each, and finally working steadily with his saw until they were all cut out. He made the end-pieces in the same way. This was all he could do the first day.

The second day he bored the holes, and then nailed the parts together. He first softened the nails, however, by heating them red-hot on a shovel in the kitchen-fire. This was not taking the temper out, as you might at first imagine, for iron cannot be hardened and tempered like steel. But most iron nails have a peculiar kind of hardness which comes from the prodigious force by which the metal is compressed in the process of manufacturing them. Heating them red-hot swells out the iron again to its natural state, and makes it soft and ductile, as it was before.

The reason why John softened his nails was so, that, when they came through on the back side of the trellis, the point might be made to turn over and clinch itself in the wood, as this would make the fastening very much stronger.

In order that the point might be thus turned over, John placed the axe on the floor, under each crossing, when he nailed it, and thus, as soon as the point of the nail came through and encountered the iron side of the axe, it was turned aside and bent over; and as John continued to strike on the head with the hammer, the point at last buried itself so completely in the wood on the under side, that it would be almost impossible to draw out the nail again, in any way, and it held the cross-piece to the side-piece, at the junction, in the firmest manner.

This process is called clinching. There is a kind of nails that are made expressly for clinching. They are already softened, and the points of them are made slender and tapering, so that they may bend over and enter the wood more easily. If you have a great deal of clinching work to do, it is best to buy clinching-nails for it; but if you have but little, you can manage it pretty well by softening a few ordinary nails for the work, as John did, by heating them in the fire.

When the trellis was finished, John painted it in a kind of lead-color, which is prepared by mixing lampblack, or some other black coloring matter, with white paint. This produces a species of neutral tint, as the painters call it, which is very suitable for such purposes. When the paint was thoroughly dry, John carried the trellis over to the house where Mary lived, and set it up there, behind her seat, where her climbing rose was growing. He first, however, made holes in the ground by means of a crow-bar, in order to make it easier to drive down the points of the side-pieces which were intended to enter the ground. When he had driven the side-pieces down to the proper depth, he rammed the earth hard around them, and thus they were made to stand very firm.

John found, on summing up the time that he had spent in making the trellis, that it amounted to four hours in all, so that Mary owed him eight dollars. She only had three, however. Part of this she had earned by helping about the pond-box, and the rest by making sails for Benny's vessels. John said that he would trust her for the rest of the money, and she said that she would earn the money and pay him the first time she could get anything to do.

She very soon found enough to do in making Benny flags and banners for his ships. She contrived a way of making them very prettily out of different colored ribbons. Benny was greatly delighted with these flags and banners, and was willing to pay any price for them, and he was quite eager to find work to do for John, so as to earn money to buy them. In a very short time Mary earned money to pay her debt, and then, though not till then, she felt that the trellis was really her own.

CHAPTER XI.

MARY'S PICTURES.

In front of the house where John and Benny lived there was a broad sidewalk, leading toward the town, which was very hard and smooth, and pretty wide; and John and Benny used often to drive their hoops and play horses there. They used to play horses and drive hoops a great deal, for it must not be supposed, from the fact that so much is said in these volumes of their mechanical operations, that they spent all their leisure time in working with tools. Far from it. In fact, they spent but a small portion of their play-hours in this way. Their mother would not allow them to spend more.

It was on account of her brother Edward's advice that she restricted them in this respect. In talking with her about it one day, he said it was an excellent thing for boys to work with tools, provided they did not work too much or too long at a time.

" If a boy works at random," said he " and without thought or care, then he will spoil what he attempts to do, and will get vexed and worried, and out of patience with his failures ; and that will do his temper and his nervous system more harm than all his exercise and practice will do good.

" If, on the other hand, he takes care and pains, then he must make many calculations, and exercise a great deal of thought, and this is very trying to the brain and whole nervous system of a boy while they are yet immature. So you had better not let John work in his shop but a small portion of the time."

Mrs. Gay, though she had not thought of this before, perceived at once that what Edward said must be true. So she made some arrangements which limited very considerably the time that John could devote to his mechanical operations, and gave him a great deal of time to play with Benny in the open air.

But to return to what I was saying.

Between the broad sidewalk, which I have described, and the garden, there was an open fence, which the children could look through when they were in the garden, and see any one passing along, either on the sidewalk or in the street. One day, when John and Benny were in the garden, their attention was attracted by a little carriage, which a girl was drawing along the sidewalk, with a baby in it, and they went up close to the fence to see. Benny looked through the openings in the fence, but John climbed up upon the fence so as to see better. While standing there, however, instead of paying attention to the little carriage and the child in it, his thoughts seemed to be occupied with something at a distance on the road.

" What is it ? " said Benny ; " what do you see ? "

" I believe cousin Mary is coming," said John.

" Is she ? " exclaimed Benny.

" Yes," said John ; " and she has got something in her hand, — something white."

John immediately climbed up higher upon the fence, so as to see better.

" Yes," said he, after looking a moment longer, " it is Mary.   She has got some papers in her hand.   Now she sees me and is running."

Before long, Mary arrived at the place where the boys were.   As she came up, though she was somewhat out of breath, she began at once to speak, saying, —

" See ! I have got some pictures for you, John. · I want you to buy them, to hang up in your shop."

The pictures were rolled up together, but Mary proceeded at once to unroll them. They were colored pictures of various kinds, representing different scenes and objects, and had originally been in a picture-book. But the book had been worn out and had come to pieces, and the pictures had lain for some time neglected in a drawer, being too pretty to be absolutely thrown away.

Mary had heard John say, a few days before, that he meant to get some pictures some time or other, and nail them up in the vacant places on the wall over his bench and at the sides of it ; and when, after going home, her eye happened to fall upon these pictures as they lay in the drawer, she said to herself, —

MARY COMING.   *Page* 110

" These are just the things for cousin
John, and I will make him buy them of
me, and so I shall get some money faster
than I can earn it by making sails, —
though I will go on making sails, too."

Mary however was well aware that it
was not proper for her to dispose even of
old and neglected pictures like these, without first obtaining her mother's permission.
So she took them to her mother and asked
the question.

" Mother," said she, " may I have these
pictures, — to do what I have a mind to
with them."

" Yes," said her mother, " you may have
them."

Mary began to look very much pleased,
when her mother suddenly added,— " That
is, I presume you may ; but it depends a
little upon what you want to do with
them."

" I want to sell them to cousin John."

" Oh, no, indeed ! " exclaimed her mother.
" I should be very unwilling to have you
do that. You may *give* the pictures to
him if you like, but I should be very unwilling to let you sell them to him for money."

Mary's countenance fell. She began to look very much disappointed. She however added, —

" Why, mother, it is only play-money."

" Oh, play-money!" repeated her mother. " That is a different thing. If it is only *play*-money, I have no objection."

" What kind of play - money is it ?" asked her mother.

. " Greenbacks," said Mary.

" Greenbacks ? " repeated her mother.

" Yes," said Mary; " some that John made."

Mary's mother seemed very much amused at the idea of John's having made greenbacks, and being about to purchase works of art with them.

" Mother," said Mary, " you need not laugh, for the greenbacks are very pretty indeed. Besides, I can get John to make things for me with them. I will show you one of them."

So Mary drew out one of the greenbacks from her pocket, and showed it to her mother. Her mother's opinion of the currency was evidently very much modified by seeing this specimen of it. She admitted

that it was very pretty money indeed, and
if, in addition to its neat and pretty appearance, it would at any time command a valuable consideration from the issuer of it,
when it was presented for redemption, it
possessed, as she could not but admit, all
the essential qualities of real money.

These were the pictures which Mary was
now bringing to show to John and Benny.
She had been very much in doubt what
price to ask for them. She finally determined upon two dollars a piece for them,
basing her judgment very properly on the
time which she imagined it would take to
make them.

" I am sure," said she to herself in reasoning on the subject, " that if a person
could draw and paint ever so well and ever
so fast, he could not make such a pretty
picture as one of these in less than an
hour; and the price of the work that John
does is two dollars an hour."

John made no objection at all to the
price which Mary fixed upon the pictures,
especially when she explained to him the
calculation and estimate on which the price
was based. There were five pictures in all.

8

John was inclined to take four of them, and let Benny have one, — Benny having said that he should like to buy one.

" Let me see," said John, as he looked at the four pictures which were left, after Benny had chosen the one which he preferred ; " if I buy these pictures for two dollars a piece, that will make eight dollars, and I shall have to work four hours to redeem the money. Now the question is, should I be willing to work four hours for these pictures ?   Yes, I should."

So he determined to pay the money.

The pictures were really very pretty ones. They had been made in Paris and colored there.   There are a great many girls in Paris who know how to color pictures most beautifully.   Some of these girls are employed all the time in coloring pictures for children's picture-books.

One of the pictures represented a prancing horse, with a man standing before him holding his head.   This was the one that Benny chose.

There was another that represented a party of boys that had been flying a kite, and the kite had got lodged among the trees, and the boys were trying to get it down by throwing up sticks and stones. Benny said he did not want *that* picture, for he did not believe the boys would ever get that kite down.

There was another one which represented a party of boys building a dam across a small brook. Some of the boys were wading about in the water, with their trousers pulled up to their knees.

There was another still, which represented a girl playing with her dolls. The girl was sitting at the head of a table at breakfast, with her two dolls on high chairs at the sides, and she was pouring out coffee for them. She was the mother, and they were her two children. One of the dolls was smaller than the other. The largest one was a girl, and the smallest was a boy. There was a very nice breakfast on the table, and the room was a very handsome one, with a pretty carpet on the floor, rich curtains at the windows, and a blazing fire in the grate.

Mary liked this picture so much that she had a great mind to keep it for herself. But on the whole she concluded to let it

go with the rest, for the sake of the two
dollars that it would bring.

"The first thing that we must do," said
John, " is to trim round the edges of the
pictures, so as to cut off the worn part, and
make them straight and square."

So the whole party proceeded at once
to the house, and passing through the yard
they went directly to John's bench, in the
back-room, and there John, taking down a
smooth board which he kept always ready
for such purposes, began to trim and square
the edges of the pictures.

Such squares as carpenters and cabinet-
makers use are not intended to be used for
sheets of paper, but only for boards and
other substances that have some considerable thickness, so that one arm of the square
may be placed in such a manner as to shut
down over the edge of it. By placing the
sheet, however, close to the edge of a board,
these squares may be used for paper, and
this was the way that John proceeded in
the present case. He soon succeeded, with
the square, and by means of a sharp-pointed
knife, in trimming off all the rough, worn,
and soiled portions of paper, near the edges,

and in thus giving the pictures a neat, symmetrical, and scientific look, which improved their appearance very much indeed.

" Now," said John, " all I have got to do is to nail them up. But first let us go and show them to mother."

CHAPTER XII.

PREPARATIONS FOR FRAMING.

John led the way into the house, followed by the two other children, and carrying the pictures in his hand to show to his mother.

Mrs. Gay was very much pleased with them when she saw them, and said they were very pretty indeed. She should like one of them herself, to hang up in her room, if it only had a frame.

" Well, mother," said John, " you can have one if you please ; only you will have to buy it. We all have to buy them, — two dollars a piece, — greenbacks."

" And if you have not got any greenbacks," said Benny, " real money will do."

Mrs. Gay looked at the pictures again. She said that they were all pretty.

" I should like one of them," she added, — " either one of John's four, and I 'll tell you what I will do. The pictures ought to be framed, and I can tell you how you can frame them. You will need some glass and also some gilt paper. You will have to buy the glass at the painter and glazier's, who will have to cut out pieces of just the right size."

" Yes," said Benny, "just as big as the pictures."

" No," replied his mother, " because there is going to be a border, and the border is going to be pasted upon the glass. So you must have the glass as large as the picture and the border together, all around. You will need gilt paper for the border. Now this is what I will do. I will pay for the glass and for the gilt paper for all five of the pictures, on condition that, after they are framed, you are to give me one of them."

" Which one ? " asked John.

" Oh, any one you please," said Mrs. Gay. " They are all pretty. I shall be satisfied with either of them."

The children at once agreed to this bargain. Mary, if she had been alone, would have been somewhat alarmed at the idea of undertaking to frame the pictures, fearing that she should not know how to do it;

but she had great faith in John's mechanical abilities, and she had no doubt that he would manage the work well.

All the pictures were of the same size, and Mrs. Gay thought that the margin of gilt paper ought to be about half an inch wide on each side.

" So," said she, " you will want a glass for each picture half an inch larger every way than the pictures themselves. The first thing is to make a pattern. You had better get a piece of pasteboard for your pattern. There are some broken pasteboard boxes up in the garret that you may have. Get a piece of this pasteboard and carry it out to your shop, and measure and mark a piece of the right size; and then you can all go to the painter's and get him to cut you out some pieces of exactly that size. He can cut them out of any of his broken panes, — only they must be clear and good glass.

" When you have got your glasses, pay him for them with the money that I shall give you, and then go to the bookstore and buy a sheet of gilt paper, the best quality that he has got. The man will roll it up for you, but you must bring it home carefully, so that it shall not get broken."

" Broken?" repeated Mary; " I never heard of paper being broken."

" Yes," said Mrs. Gay. " All paper is covered on each side with a thin film of *sizing*, as they call it, like a kind of varnish, and this can get broken; and when it is once broken by rough handling of the paper, it can never be made to look really smooth and nice again.

" In the same manner," continued Mrs. Gay, " the films of gold leaf upon the paper may be broken apart in some places, and then they never can be joined together again, so as to make the paper look as it did before.

" Bring the glass and paper to me when you come home, and then I will tell you how to proceed in framing the pictures."

So Mrs. Gay gave the children some money, and they all set off together to go into town, — after having first procured the pasteboard and made their pattern. They left the pictures all safe upon one of the shelves of John's lockup while they were gone.

They went first to the painter's, — for painters are almost always glaziers too. The paint-shop was not very large, and it seemed to be full of pots of paint, and barrels of oil and varnish, and little kegs full of colors, and bundles of brushes, and other such things. There was a short counter, and behind it some shelves which were divided by partitions into little bins, which contained panes of glass of all sizes. In some of the bins were broken pieces of glass, the fragments of large panes which had become accidentally cracked or broken.

There was only a boy in the shop when the children came in, and when John told him what they wanted, he immediately took down some of the broken panes of glass and tried them with the pattern, in order to find pieces from which he could cut out what John required. He found them very easily, and laying them down, one after another, on a broad board which lay upon the counter, and which was ruled curiously with black lines, by means of which he could cut out the glass to any measure. He had first laid down the pattern on this board, to ascertain the exact size of it, by means of these lines.

It is very curious to see a glazier cut glass by means of his diamond. The diamond is very small indeed — not so big usually as the head of a pin.

This precious little point is fastened securely into a brass socket, at the end of a curious kind of handle. The lower end of the handle is made square, and has one smooth side intended to slide along the edge of a ruler when the glazier is cutting with it. This lower end moves a little too, on a pivot, so as always to keep the sharp point in the piece of diamond which is meant to do the cutting in the right position, as the glazier moves it along.

The glazier boy laid the broken pane of glass down upon his board, in the right place, and then, taking the handle of the diamond between two of his fingers, he drew a line along the glass. The diamond made a slight scratching sound as it moved along, — though, after all, it was not a scratch, but a *fissure* that it made in the glass.

That is, (and this is something very curious, and extremely difficult to explain,) the diamond does not merely make a *mark* on the surface of the glass, as you do when

you scratch a board with a pin, or with the
point of a knife, but it actually cracks the
glass down nearly through to the under
side, in the exact line along which the
point of the diamond runs, so that the
glass will afterward break apart in that
place very easily. It does not crack entirely through, but only *almost* through.

Thus there are two things very curious
about the diamond. There is nothing at
all surprising in the fact that it will scratch
the glass, being, as it is, so extremely
hard; but it is very surprising that it
should *crack* it nearly through, and still
more curious that, since it cracks it nearly
through, it does not crack it *entirely*
through.

This fact that the diamond causes a fissure to run along the glass almost through
to the under side, is what makes it so
valuable for this purpose. You can *scratch*
glass with a piece of flint, or with the
sharp corner of a broken file; but to cause
a fissure to run deep into the substance of
the glass, along any particular line, so as
to cause it to come in two there, easily
and certainly, requires a diamond.

When the glazier boy had cut out the five pieces of glass, he said the price to be paid for them was fifteen cents, that is, three cents a piece. John paid the money, and the boy wrapped up the little panes in a paper, having first put a separate piece of paper between every two panes, to diminish the danger of their being broken in carrying, — and then the children, taking them, went away.

They proceeded next to the bookstore to buy the gilt paper. They found that there were several different qualities of gilt paper. There was one kind which was very cheap, and another which was quite dear. The bookseller told them that the cheap kind, though called *gilt* paper, was not covered with real gold, but with what they call Dutch gold, — which was in fact a kind of tinsel or brass, and though it looked very well at first, would tarnish after a while, when exposed to the air.

So, finding that they had money enough, the children decided on buying a sheet of the best kind. The bookseller rolled it up carefully, and John gave it to Mary to carry, thinking that it would be most safe in her hands.

As soon as the children had returned home, they proceeded at once to what Mrs. Gay called the first stage of the work of framing the pictures, which was that of cutting out the parts. They were only to undertake that first stage, she said, on that day.

The idea of the children was, that the first day's work would consist of framing a certain number of pictures, having a notion that they would work upon one and finish it before they commenced upon another. But Mrs. Gay told them that that was not the way. All the pictures must be carried along together, she said. That was not only the easiest, but also the surest way.

So that all that they could do the first day was to cut out the *pieces* which would be required.

" The pieces you will need," said she, " are of three kinds, — first, backs ; second, wings ; third, fronts.

" You will need five backs, one for each picture.

" You will need ten wings, two for each picture.

" You will need twenty fronts, four for each picture.

" The backs," continued Mrs. Gay, " are to be pieces of pasteboard, each one to be of exactly the size of the piece of glass that it is to go with. Of course you must have five of them.

" The wings are pieces of cotton cloth, about one inch wide, and just as long as the longest side of the glass. These are for bindings, to bind the glass and the pasteboard back together after the picture has been put in between them. You will want two for each glass, and of course you will want ten of them.

" The fronts are the strips of gold paper, which are to form the border for the frame. They must be about an inch wide, and two for each picture must be as long as the picture is long, and the two others as long as the picture is wide. Of course you will want twenty of them.

" Go and cut all these pieces out, and then lay all your work carefully away, and some other day, when Mary comes, I will tell you how to put them together."

The children did all this work as their mother had directed. They found boxes in the garret from which they procured pasteboard for the backs. Their mother gave them some cotton cloth for what she called the wings; and the gilt paper, for the fronts, they had. John cut out the backs and the fronts, while Mary, with a sharp pair of scissors, cut out the wings, — though why her aunt called them wings she could not understand. John also cut the sheet of gilt paper into strips an inch wide, by means of a ruler and a smooth board.

Each of these strips he found was long enough to make one side and one end of a picture, so that with ten strips cut off lengthwise of the sheet he made the whole twenty fronts; and then, much to his satisfaction, he had more than half his sheet of gilt paper left over, to be used on some other occasion.

" Next time we make a kite, Benny," said he, " we will have some golden stars upon it."

" So we will," said Benny.

When all the pieces were thus prepared, Mary washed the glasses nicely, and then they laid everything away carefully in a drawer, pictures and all, and there they remained several days.

CHAPTER XIII.

IMPROVEMENT IN THE POND.

THE children intended, on the day when they made their preparations for framing their pictures, to finish the work on the following day ; but Mrs. Gay preferred that they should not do so. She knew very well that too much nice work of this kind — requiring close calculations, and careful attention to minute points, and other such efforts as these, which tax the mind and brain rather than the muscles and the limbs — is not good for children who are growing. So, without absolutely forbidding them to finish their work, she thought she would endeavor to divert their attention from it.

Accordingly, after John came home from school that day and was beginning to think at dinner-time what he should do that afternoon, she said to the boys that ſur would like to go out after dinner ar you

9

their pond again, and see what new boats Benny had got.

Benny was very much pleased with this idea.

" Only, mother," said he, " you must wait a few minutes after dinner till we have time to fill up our pond. The water all goes off when we leave it, and we have to pump it full every day when we are going to sail our boats."

" What is the reason of that ? " asked Mrs. Gay.

" John says it leaks," replied Benny. " But I don't see how it can leak, for John made the joints very tight indeed."

" Yes ; but he could not make them tight enough not to leak somewhat," said Mrs. Gay. "And if all the cracks leak a little,— since there are so many of them, and they are such long ones, — the whole amount of leakage must be very large. Can't you stop up the cracks in some way ? "

" We covered the bottom all over with sand," said John. " We thought that would stop up the cracks."

the " That helped, no doubt," said his moth-
drawe but sand is too pervious to water."
mained

" What does that mean ? " asked John.

" It means that it lets the water run through it," said Mrs. Gay. " You must cover the bottom with something that is *im*pervious to water, — that is, which will not let the water through."

" And what is there ? " asked John.

" Clay," replied his mother. " Clay is impervious to water. You might plaster over the whole bottom of your pond with clay, and that I suppose would make it nearly tight, — but it would be a very dirty job."

" Oh, I should not care about that," said John.

" Nor I," said Benny, — " not a bit."

" No," rejoined Mrs. Gay ; " it is *I* that should care about that, on account of your clothes. But perhaps you could find some old clothes to put on."

" We can, mother," said John ; " there are plenty of them in the garret."

" You had better first go and see Eben-ezer," said Mrs. Gay, " and hear what he will say about it. If he thinks that a lin-ing of clay is the best thing to make your pond tight, and if Wilmot can tell you where you can get some clay, and if also you can find some old clothes to wear while you are doing the job, then you may try and see what you can do."

So the boys determined at once to go off and find Ebenezer. They did not expect to find him at the house, for it was a pleasant day, and it was haying-time. So they thought that he would be in the field.

Very fortunately, however, when the boys arrived at the house, they found that Ebenezer had just finished unloading a load of hay, and was going back to the field with the empty cart. So he asked them to climb in and ride with him, and on the way they stated their case to him, and heard what he had to say.

I cannot relate in full all the conversation that took place. It will be sufficient to give the substance of it. Ebenezer explained to them three modes of making the seams in a box like their pond-box tight.

The first mode was by what he called caulking them. This is the method which is adopted in the case of boats and vessels. The workmen first open the seams wider by driving wedges in, which crowds the wood out upon one side and the other of the crack, and compresses it a great deal. But the boards or planks must be nailed on very strong, and with a great many nails, and the frame-work of the boat must be very solid to bear this wedging open of the seams. If they are not so, instead of compressing the wood merely, the wedges would force the boards apart, and thus greatly enlarge the seams, and so make the boat leak worse than ever.

When the seams are properly opened, then the caulkers fill them all up again by driving in oakum, which is a kind of tarred hemp, made by picking open bits of rope and cordage of all kinds. The caulkers drive this tarred hemp into all the seams as hard as they can drive it, and the wood which has been compressed swells back again when it becomes wet, and pinches the oakum so tight that not a particle of water can find its way through.

Ebenezer said that this was the surest way to make seams tight; but that they could not adopt it with their box, for it was not made strong enough to bear it.

John said that his box was made pretty strong. Ebenezer said that he did not doubt it was made pretty strong for a box. But no box could be strong enough to bear caulking, unless it was made upon a solid frame, and nailed to it in every part in the firmest manner.

The next best plan to make a box tight, Ebenezer said, was to line the inside of it with mortar made of hydraulic cement. That would be very easily done, and it would be very permanent and sure; but it would cost too much money. John would have to buy a barrel of cement, he said, and that would cost several dollars.

Then came the last plan, which was to line the inside of the box with clay, as Mrs. Gay had suggested; and this, Ebenezer said, he thought was on the whole much the best plan.

He said that the boys could get some clay at the brick-yard, and wheel it home on their wheelbarrow.

" The drier it is," said he, " the lighter it will be, and the more you can haul at a load. Then you can break it in the box, and make a kind of mortar of it there, and

cover the whole bottom of the box with
the mortar, and bank it up all around the
sides.   You can make some trowels out of
shingles, or of very thin boards, to plaster
it on with.

" Then, after it is done, you can cover
the clay all over with sand, to make a
clean and pretty bottom to the pond."

The boys determined to carry this plan
into effect.   So they went home, and after
reporting what Ebenezer had told them to
their mother, they went up into the garret
and found some clothes there, worn and
ragged, which had belonged to John a year
or two ago.   Besides being all worn out,
they were altogether too small now for
John, and at the same time too big for
Benny.   However, both the boys rigged
themselves out in them, and then came
down-stairs, each one laughing at the ab-
surd figure which the other made.   Even
their mother could not help smiling when
she came to see them.

Dressed in this ridiculous toggery, the
boys took their wheelbarrow and a small
shovel, and proceeded along by a back road
which led to a brick-yard in the rear of the
town.

The boys expected that even the bricklayers would laugh at them, but they did
not. Indeed, the bricklayers did not look
much better themselves. They told the
men that they wanted to get some clay,
and the men showed them a place where
they might take as much as they liked
from a heap of clods which had been
thrown out as refuse.

These clods were of all shapes and sizes,
and were nearly dry. So the boys loaded
their wheelbarrow with them, and wheeled
the load home. When they got there they
threw the lumps of clay off into the pond-
box, and then went for another load. In
this way they went to and fro, five or six
times, until they were sure that they had
brought enough.

Then John brought an axe, and Benny
his mallet, and with these implements they
broke the lumps of clay to pieces, and made
them as fine as they could. Then John
went and pumped a little water in, enough
to spread over the bottom of the box and
moisten the clay. When this was done,
the boys took off their stockings and shoes,
and got into the box, and began trampling

about among the clay to mix it more completely with the water. It soon began to assume the appearance of mortar. They also got two long round sticks of wood, that were sawed off square at the end, and used these to mash up the lumps of clay with, until at length, after the lapse of about an hour, the clay was well mixed with the water, and the whole was reduced to one homogeneous mass, — that is, to a mass that was all alike in every part.

It is true that by this time the boys had made themselves very muddy, and had spattered themselves well from head to foot; but this was of no consequence, as the clothes which they wore were of no value.

At length, when the mortar, as they called it, was all ready, John went and made two wooden trowels out of some shingles that he had in his shop, and he and Benny spread the mortar smoothly over the whole bottom of the box, and banked it up against the sides in such a manner that at last they had, as it were, a shallow basin of clay set within a wooden box.

" Now," said John, " we can take off
these old dirty clothes."

The boys, in fact, had by this time become tired of their clothes. There is fun,
and there is also discomfort, in wearing old,
ragged, and muddy clothes. The fun is
great at first, but goes on gradually dimin-
ishing. The discomfort, on the other hand,
is not felt much at first, but goes on in-
creasing. At least John and Benny found
it so in this case, and by the time that their
work was done the discomfort began to
predominate greatly over the fun.

So they washed their faces and hands at
the pump, and then went up into the garret and put on their proper clothes again,
hanging the muddy ones up to dry.

They then returned to the pond, and
with the wheelbarrow brought a number of
loads of fresh sand, and covered all the clay
up several inches deep, so that their pond
might have a clean and pretty bottom.
When this was done, they pumped the
pond full of water, and Benny put his
boats in again. They found, after this,
that the pond held its water very well.
After it was once filled, it remained full

for several days, though the water gradually wasted away by evaporation from
the surface.   But the clay answered the
purpose for which it was intended so well
that there was scarcely any leakage through
the bottom at all.

CHAPTER XIV.

FRAMING THE PICTURES.

I WILL now tell you how John and Mary proceeded to finish framing their pictures; for Benny, although he took great interest in the operation, did not do much about it, except to stand by and look on, and be ready to help when he could, by handing to John or Mary what they wanted.

Mrs. Gay had given them full instructions how to proceed, and they followed the instructions precisely.

One of the most important of the instructions was, that when they commenced upon the work they must carry on all the pictures together, instead of taking one at a time and first finishing that completely, and then beginning upon another.

The principle, " one thing at a time," — which is a most excellent one in respect to many things, — does not apply to the case of mechanical operations, where you have

many things of the same kind to make.
Here the principle is modified and becomes
one *operation* at a time. That is, it is
much better to carry the work all on together, by performing one operation on all
the pieces at the same time, and then taking the next operation for all the pieces,
until all the work is done. You will see
how John and Mary followed this rule in
working upon the pictures.

In accordance with his mother's instructions, then, John first put his glue-pot down
by the kitchen-fire to heat the glue, and by
the side of it, though in a much hotter
place, a brick.

The hot brick was to keep the glue warm
while he was using it on his bench. For
glue cannot be used except when it is hot,
and John was not allowed to have any fire
at his bench. So, when he was going to
work with his glue for some time, he used
to have a hot brick to set the glue-pot
upon, and this kept it in good condition
a long while.

Then the children went all together to
John's bench. They took the work out of
the cupboard, and, after having carefully

swept off the bench, they arranged the pieces in order.

They placed the five pieces of pasteboard which were to form the backs of the pictures in a row, near the front part of the bench, with the pictures upon them, — each picture on its own pasteboard. Behind them, in another row, they placed the glasses, and also the wings, and the front strips, so that each set should be by itself. Things being thus arranged, they were prepared to commence their work.

" Now," said John, " the first thing for me to do is to find exactly where these pictures are to come, on the pasteboard, — that is to say, exactly in the middle; and then you must gum them there."

The reader will recollect that the pasteboards and the glasses were made a half an inch larger each way than the pictures, in order to allow space for the border. Of course the pictures were now to be fastened to their pasteboard backs exactly in the middle of them, so as to leave the proper space for the border all around.

John proceeded at once to measure for this. He laid the first picture down upon its pasteboard as near the middle as he could, and then with the compasses measured the margin on each side, and then slipped the paper one way or the other until he found that the spaces on each side were equal. Then he made little marks with a pencil at the edge of the picture on each side, as a guide to Mary, after which he measured and marked in the same way the distances at the top and bottom.

" Now," said John, " gum the picture by the four corners on the pasteboard just where I have marked it. Put the least possible touch of gum, not so big as the head of a pin, on the under side, at the four corners ; and when you have placed the picture exactly where it is to go, put the glass on it, to keep it down flat until it is dry."

While Mary was doing this, John passed on to the next picture in the same way, and then to the next and the next, until he had marked them all. It was plainly much better to do all this work of adjustment together, while his mind was upon it, and he had the compasses and the pencil in his hand.

Indeed, he went along the row very rapidly, and had them all marked in almost as little time as it has taken me to tell how he did it.

Mary followed almost as fast. She gummed the pictures on the under side a very little, with thick gum which she obtained from a little bottle which she had brought out with her for the purpose. There must be very little gum used in such a case, and that must be very thick, or else it will wet the paper and swell it; and then, when it is dry, the paper will shrink unequally, and draw the margin of the picture out of shape. The gum in this case was not for the purpose of holding the picture down, since the glass which was to be put over it would do that, — but only to keep it from slipping about there, and getting out of place, — and a very little gum would be sufficient for that purpose. John said that Mary must put on a quantity no bigger than the head of a pin; but what you could take up on the very extreme *point* of a pin would have been enough, if Mary could have put on so little.

" Now," said John, " the next thing is to

glue on the wings; and I must go in and get the glue."

So he took a short board in his hand and went to the kitchen-fire to get the glue. He laid the board down upon the hearth, and with the tongs put the hot brick upon it. Then he put the glue-pot upon the brick, and taking up the board at the two ends, he brought all together out to the bench.

The first thing that he did was to turn the first picture over, bottom upwards, having however previously put a piece of smooth newspaper down upon the bench, to prevent soiling the picture. Then taking his glue-brush, which was quite a small one, so that he could work very neatly with it, he dipped it in the glue, and then drew it carefully along the left-hand border of the first pasteboard, so as to cover a strip there about half an inch wide with the glue, taking care to lay it on smooth and thin in every part. Mary stood by with one of the wings — that is, the narrow strips of cotton cloth — in her hand, all ready to give to John to put on, while she at the same time took the brush from him. John im-

mediately applied the wing by one of its
edges to the glued part of the pasteboard,
and pressed it down along its whole length
by patting it with a towel.

As the wing was an inch wide, and the
glued strip upon the pasteboard was only
half an inch wide, the wing projected beyond the pasteboard about half an inch.

In the same manner John glued the wing
on the other side, and then turning the
picture over again, and laying it flat on its
back, he and Mary saw the two side-pieces
which he had attached to it projecting each
way about half an inch, forming as it were
a pair of wings.

" Ah! now I see what aunt meant by
calling them wings," said Mary. " They
are wings."

" Yes; but they won't be wings long,"
said John; " for we are going pretty soon
to glue them over upon the glass; and they
won't be able to do much flying after
that."

After having thus put on the wings to
the first picture, John proceeded to all the
others in succession, and performed the
same operation upon them all.

" Now," said he, " for the glasses. And before we put them on, we must make sure that they are perfectly clean — especially the under side ; for we can never get at them on that side, to clean them, after the wings are glued down over them."

So Mary went into the house, and brought out a clean towel. The glasses had been washed before, but they had since then been touched and handled a little, and accordingly Mary wiped them again very carefully, and then laid them down, one by one, over its picture. Thus the pictures formed a row, regularly arranged along the bench, with the pasteboard backs downward upon the bench, and the pictures upon them, each in the exact centre of its own pasteboard, the glasses over the pictures, and the wings of cotton cloth extending out about half an inch each side.

" How pretty they are going to look," said Benny.

" Yes," said John; " but don't touch them for your life."

Benny, to make sure of not touching them, kept his hands behind him ; but he looked at them, one after another, very

attentively, and seemed to admire them
very much.

" Now," said John, " the next thing is to
glue the wings down over the glass, in
order to fasten the glass and picture and
back all together."

So he proceeded to draw his brush —
previously filled with glue — along the
margin of the glass, first on one side and
then on the other, and then to fold down
the wings on each side over the places, —
drawing the cloth over tight, so as to bind
the glass and the pasteboard firmly together.
He could do this very safely, for while he
had been gluing the wings upon the other
pasteboards, those attached to the first one
had in a great measure dried, so that they
held well.

After the wings had thus been all glued
down, nothing remained but to put on the
borders of gilt paper all around the glass,
on the upper side. This was in some
respects the most delicate operation of all.
It is a pretty nice business to put strips of
gilt paper neatly around a picture, for a
border, especially if you have to do it with
glue which, as it cannot be used except

while it is hot, requires that the workman should proceed with considerable dispatch, — but still in a very calm and quiet manner, — in laying down the paper in its place as soon as the glue has been applied to it.

Glue, too, when it is used for gluing paper in this way, must be much thinner than when it is used for gluing wood, else it cannot be spread smoothly and evenly over the paper. To make his glue thin enough, John poured some hot water into it from the little kettle below, and stirred it up with the brush until he had made it quite thin, so that it would flow easily and smoothly over the paper.

Then he spread down a quarter of a newspaper on the bench by the side of the first picture, and laying down one of the strips of gilt paper upon it, with the gilt side down, he washed the other side all over with the diluted glue. Then, immediately taking it up, he applied it carefully along one side of the glass over the part where the wing had been glued down. He laid it on in such a manner as that the inner edge of it should come close to the margin of the picture, while the other edge extended a little beyond the edge of the glass, so that he could fold it over the edge, and let it lap a little upon the back side. He did the same with the strip on the other side.

Both the strips had been made a little longer than the glass, so as to furnish ends to take hold of. When the strips had been put on and well patted down, Mary trimmed off these ends with her scissors, and the *side*-borders were then complete.

John proceeded in this way regularly until the side-borders of all the five pictures were put on. He remained in the same place while he did all this gluing, Mary bringing him the pictures one after another to have the borders put on, and then carrying them back and laying them down carefully in their places.

Then came the end-borders.

Now, in respect to the end-borders there is something to be done, to make a proper finish at the corners, which it is rather difficult to explain; for to make the frame look right, the last set of borders ought to be *mitred*.

But perhaps you do not know what *mitring* means.

A mitre is a joining of two things together at an angle of forty-five degrees.

But perhaps you do not know any better what this joining things together at an angle of forty-five degrees means.

I will tell you how John did it — following the instructions which his mother had given him.

When one of the end-pieces was properly brushed over with glue, and laid down carefully in its place, John patted it down in the middle, but left the ends lying loosely in their places. Then he lifted up the ends, first one and then the other, and cut them off in a slanting direction, beginning exactly at the corner of the glass, which was of course the outer corner of the border, and cutting in a diagonal direction, exactly to the *inner* corner. He was careful to get the scissors in exactly the right position before he cut, and then, when he had made the cut, he patted the end of the piece down in its place. He did the same at all the four corners, and it made a very pretty finish. Such a joint as this is called a mitre. Almost all looking-glasses and picture-frames are finished in this way, as you will easily see. So are usually the mouldings about the pannels of doors; but not the outer framework of the door, which encloses the pannels.

After these borders had been all put on, the fronts of the pictures were finished. There was something still to be done to the backs, especially putting on two ribbons behind to hang the pictures up by.

The children used for this purpose some narrow pink ribbon, with which Mrs. Gay furnished them. They were cut into the proper lengths, and one was appropriated to each picture. John first put a little glue with his brush on the back of the picture, — that is, upon the pasteboard, near each of the upper corners, — and then laid down one end of the ribbon upon each place, and patted it down. About an inch of each end of the ribbon was thus glued to the back of the picture, near the two upper corners. Of course John measured and marked, so as to get these points of attachment at the same distance from the corner on each side.

Then, for the last thing, the children cut
out some sheets of marble - paper, which
Mrs. Gay gave them, taking care to make
them of the right size to almost cover the
backs of the pictures, leaving just a little
peep of the gilt paper all around the margin. This marble-paper covered the ends
of the ribbon, where they were glued on,
and made the back look neat and finished.

When the pictures were all done, John
piled them up in a pile upon the bench
near the window, putting a smooth thin
board between each two, and then put
something rather heavy upon the top board,
but not heavy enough to break the glasses.
This was to keep the pasteboards and the
pictures, and also the gilt borders, all
smooth and flat while they were drying.

Here they were left without being dis-
turbed until the next day. By this time
they were thoroughly dry, so that they
could be safely handled. They looked extremely well when they were taken out,
and the children were very much pleased
with them. They carried them all into the
house to show them to Mrs. Gay, and to
give her the one which was to be hers.

They offered her her choice, but she said
that they were all so pretty that John might
take the two that he pleased, and she would
have the other.

So the pictures were divided amicably,
and every one was satisfied. Benny hung
his up in his bedroom near his bed. John
hung his against the wall over his bench.
Mrs. Gay set up hers upon the mantel-
shelf in the sitting-room, and Mary carried
hers home to show it to her mother, and to
her little sister Luly.

CHAPTER XV.

QUITE A CARPENTER.

In the course of the summer, John undertook and completed quite a number of works of different kinds, which cannot, however, be particularly described here. He only worked in his shop in stormy days when he could not play out-of-doors. His mother preferred that when it was pleasant he and Benny should amuse themselves in the open air.

He at one time formed the plan of building a summer-house in an elevated part of the garden where there was a fine view. He intended to have the summer-house covered with creepers and vines, so as to form a sort of bower where his mother could go and sit and read, if she chose, or even sew, in sunny weather. But his mother did not encourage this plan, for she had observed, that, however charming, in a poetical sense, the idea of an arbor or a vine-clad bower might be, such places were in point of fact usually far more favorite places of resort for spiders and caterpillars than for lady occupants.

She said, however, that, if John would make a *seat* there, and a good-sized trellis behind the seat, at the distance of a few feet, to keep off the morning sun, and perhaps two other trellises at the sides for wings, — all, however, to be at such a distance from the seat that there should be no danger from insects, — it might be a very good plan.

So John made the drawings for a seat and trellises on this idea. He found, however, on making a calculation of the number of pieces which would be required, and the amount of labor necessary, that it would not be possible for him to complete such a work that summer, and he determined to reserve it for fall and winter, on days when it would be too cold to play out-of-doors, but not too cold to saw and plane in his shop.

And he did really make the trellises and the seat during the next fall and winter, and he put them up early in the spring.

Wilmot then made a rich bed behind each of the trellises, and planted climbing plants and runners in them, so that before the next summer was half gone the trellises were covered with foliage, and the seat became a very pleasant place.

It is true that Mrs. Gay did not often go out with her book or her work, and sit upon this seat to read or to sew, but very frequently, when she had visitors and they went out to walk in the garden, or upon the grounds, the company would often stop to rest themselves upon this seat, and view the surrounding scenery.

John made one thing in the course of the summer which pleased Benny and his little cousin Luly, Mary's sister, very much indeed, and that was a rocking-boat. Mary had asked him some time before whether he could not make her a rocking-horse, as perhaps my readers will recollect; and they may also recollect that he replied that he might possibly make the rockers, but he did not think that he could make any horse.

It finally occurred to John that he might set a *box* upon a pair of rockers, and call it

a rocking-boat; and this was the plan that
he finally carried into execution.

He resorted to quite an ingenious con-
trivance for drawing the curve to which the
rockers were to be cut.   He first chose a
board of about a foot in width to make the
rockers of, and sawed off two lengths from
it, each four feet long.   He laid down one
of these boards upon the floor, and then going off to a distance of three or four feet,
exactly opposite to the middle of it, he
drove a small nail into the floor.   As the
floor was a rough one, such as is generally
used in sheds and out-buildings, this did no
damage.

He then took a long twine, and making
a loop in one end of it, he slipped the loop
over the nail, and then going with the other
end to the board, he drew it tight to the
farther edge of the board.   Here he wound
the twine around the pencil.   Thus the
twine kept the pencil always at the same
distance from the nail, and by moving the
point of the pencil to the right and left
along the board he described the arc of a
circle upon it, from the nail as a centre.
He then screwed this board in his vice, and

with the shave he cut away the wood on the lower edge of it, to this mark, and so gave to the edge of the board the form of a rocker.

When this board was finished, he used it as a pattern to make the other rocker by, and so he had a pair of rockers.

He then nailed two narrow boards across from one of these rockers to the other, on the upper edge of them, and another broader one in the middle, setting the broad one up edgewise so as to brace the rockers apart, as it were, and hold them stiff in their proper vertical position. This made what might be called a rocking-frame; and though of course there was no convenient place to sit upon it, Benny could not wait to have the top made and put on, but seemed to have a great desire to get upon the frame and rock himself upon it, to and fro, notwithstanding the extremely uncomfortable position he must have been in.

In due time, however, John made a sort of box, with pretty high ends, and low sides for convenience of getting in, and two seats on the inside, one at each end.

This he fastened upon the rocking-frame so as to make what he called a rocking boat. Benny and Luly used to get into this boat, and rock themselves a great deal. They thought it was the best thing that John ever made.

The box of this rocking-boat was made to extend over the rockers on each side nearly eight inches. This was a plan which Ebenezer suggested in order that the rocks, being thus well under the box, and out of the way, the children could not get their toes under them when standing near.

John was so careful about his work and his tools, that he very seldom met with any accident in any of his operations. One accident nevertheless occured during the building of the rocking-boat, which however very fortunately led to no serious consequences. It seems, that, after he had drawn his circular arc upon the board by means of the nail in the floor and the twine, he forgot to draw out the nail after he had done using it, and Benny, in running about there afterward, tripped over it and tumbled down. He was somewhat hurt, and more frightened; and he made at first a loud outcry. John however soon succeeded in quieting him, and then drew out the nail.

Besides, these John made several other things in the course of this summer; but there is not room to describe them all here.

11

CHAPTER XVI.

SHIP-BUILDING.

ALTHOUGH it is generally a fine thing, when working with carpenter's tools, to take a great deal of pains, and do everything in the most perfect manner, so that what you make shall have a real and lasting value, still sometimes, when you are aiming at only some temporary purpose, a great deal of pleasure may be afforded by means of work very hastily and slightly done.

An illustration of this occurred one day in the case of a fleet of vessels which John made for Benny, and which he and Benny sent to sea on long voyages, from which they never returned.

Toward the end of the summer, — I believe it was in the very last week of August, — John and Benny were sitting one day together upon a seat in the garden, when they heard a rumbling sound, as of distant thunder. They looked toward the west, and then they saw a range of rounded masses of clouds, rising up into the sky. These clouds were of the kind the boys call thunder-heads. They were of a dark color in general, though the upper margins of them were here and there of a silvery brightness, which was caused by the rays of the sun reflected from them. Below they passed into a uniform expanse of cloud, which was very dark indeed, and which extended all along the western horizon.

It was from this lower expanse of gathering blackness that the sound of thunder appeared to come.

" There ! " said Benny, " I hear it again."

" Yes," said John ; " we are going to have a thunder-shower, and I am glad of it."

" What for ? " asked Benny.

" Because then we shall have a ride to-morrow," replied John. " Mother has been planning an excursion out to Warner's Pond. She said she was going the first cool day after a rain, so that the roads should not be dusty.

" There ! " said Benny ; " it thunders again. Pretty soon it will begin to lighten."

" It has lightened already," replied John. " It always lightens when it thunders, and it always thunders when it lightens."

" No," rejoined Benny, " for it thundered just now, and it did not lighten at all."

" Yes," said John, " it lightened where the thunder was, but we could not see it because it is such bright daylight all around us. We can never see any light that is a great way off, in bright daylight. We cannot see the stars in the daytime."

" There *are* no stars in the daytime," said Benny.

" Yes," replied John, " there are as many stars in the daytime as there are in the night, only we can't see them."

" Oh, John ! " exclaimed Benny. He was quite surprised to hear John make so extraordinary an assertion.

" Yes," continued John, " the stars stay in the sky all the daytime, just as they do in the night, — only we can't see them, because the air is so bright."

Here Benny gazed long and earnestly into the sky, but he could not detect the faintest semblance of a star, and finally said that if there were any stars there, he was very sure that he could see them.

Just then there came a louder peal of thunder, and the boys saw Wilmot gathering up his garden-tools and putting them into the wheelbarrow as if he was going in. So they thought they would go in too; but instead of going into the house they went to John's shop, and sat down upon a bench there, before the door which looked out into the yard.

" We will stay here," said John, " until the lightning gets too near, and then we will go into the house."

" How can we tell when it gets too near ? " asked Benny. " By the brightness ? "

" No," replied John, " not altogether by the brightness, but by the flash of lightning and the clap of thunder coming near together. The nearer they come together, the nearer the lightning is to us; and when they begin to come pretty close together, then we will go into the house."

" Is it any safer for us in the house than it is out here ? " asked Benny.

" No," said John; " we shall be just as

likely to be struck there as here. Still I would rather go in, for if I am going to be struck by lightning at all, I would rather be by mother when it happens."

" John," said Benny, after a short pause, " I don't believe there are any stars in the sky in the daytime, because there would not be any use in it."

" Then where do you think they come from — so many of them, " asked John — " every evening, as soon as the sun goes down ? "

" Why they come *out* — somehow," said John. " You see they don't light them till it begins to get dark."

Just then the clouds, which had been rapidly rising and growing very dense and dark overhead, began suddenly to pour down a shower of large drops which rattled upon the roof over where the boys were sitting, almost like hail.

" Ah ha ! " exclaimed John, in a tone of great satisfaction. " Do you hear that ? We shall have our excursion to-morrow, you may depend."

" Is Warner's Pond a good place to sail boats in ? " asked Benny.

" Yes," said John, " excellent. And right behind the tavern, where we are going to stop for dinner, is a beautiful smooth beach for us to stand upon, while we are sailing them."

" Then," said Benny, " I wish you would make me a boat, or a vessel, and let me carry it there in the carriage and sail it."

"Very well," said John. " I 'll make you two or three vessels; and I 'll do it now while it 's raining and thundering."

So saying, John proceeded to his bench, and looking under it he selected from the blocks and small pieces of wood which were stored there, three pieces which he thought were of the right size. They were about a foot long and four inches wide.

" You see I am going to make you some very big vessels," said he. " Because when you send them off a-sailing they will go away out into the middle of the pond, if the wind is fair, and if I make them pretty big we can see them a long time."

" Yes," said Benny, " I should like to have them as big as you can make them."

John took one of his boards and screwed it into his vice in such a position that with a certain tool that he had he could shave off one of the front corners of the board, so as to form one of the bows of the vessel. When he had done this, he turned the board over and fashioned the other bow. He also afterward shaved the sides away a little in a tapering direction, toward the stern, so as to give the board the shape of the deck of a vessel.

" There," said he, surveying it with a look of satisfaction, after he had finished this work. " There! That will do for one."

" Now you must bore the hole for the mast," said Benny.

" No," said John. " I must shape all my other vessels first. One thing at a time is the rule, and that means one operation at a time, not one vessel at a time."

So saying, John laid his first vessel aside and took the next one and shaped that in the same way.

" What do they call this kind of a cutter that you are cutting with ? " asked Benny.

" They call it a draw-shave," replied John. " They call it a shave, because we shave with it; and they call it a draw-shave, because we shave with it by drawing, or pulling it, toward us."

After shaping all three of the vessels, John put the draw-shave away.

" Now for the holes for the masts," said Benny.

" No," said John ; " now for the masts themselves. I shall make the masts first, and then choose a borer to fit them."

So John looked under his bench again and brought out some slender sticks, and with his fore-plane planed them to the right size, and then rounded them.

He might have done this work, too, with the draw-shave pretty well, if he had been sure that his strips of wood were perfectly straight-grained. If the wood is not perfectly straight-grained, the shaving made by a draw-shave is apt to run in or out, following the grain ; whereas that made by a plane is cut straight, the plane being kept in a perfectly straight course by the under surface of it, as it slides along.

John soon finished his three masts, for he determined to make only three, — intending to have all his vessels sloop-rigged. When the masts were finished, he selected a proper borer, and began to bore the holes.

" Now, Benny," said he, " we need some stiff white paper to make the sails of. You must go in and ask mother to give us some."

So Benny went in and presently returned with a large sheet of pretty stiff white wrapping-paper, of the kind called cartridge-paper. John, who had by this time finished making the holes, began to cut out the sails. He made them all alike and of the form of the main-sail of a sloop, that is rather narrow at the top and wider at the bottom, — the outer lower corner forming a point which he said the main-sheet was to be fastened to.

Then he cut a row of holes along pretty near to the straight side of the sail, intend-ing to pass the mast through these holes, in and out. This could be easily done, as each mast was made tapering nearly to a point at the top. Then he fastened a thread, which he called the main-sheet, to the outer lower corner of each sail.

" Now," said he, " when I draw the main-sheets aft and fasten them to the belaying-pins, the sails will hold the wind."

So saying, he drove two small tacks in the wood at the sides of each vessel, near the stern, — one on the starboard side, and the other on the larboard. These, he said, were the belaying-pins.

"Now," said John, "they are all finished."

"Except the rudders," rejoined Benny. "We must have some rudders."

"No," said John; "we shall have to do without rudders. And we shall not need rudders very much, for I have set the masts so far forward that the sails will keep the vessels right before the wind, and that is all the way we expect to sail them."

Benny did not understand this very well, but since John said so, he had no doubt but that it was all right.

"Now," said John, "we will take the vessels to pieces and pack them up."

"Who ever heard of taking vessels to pieces and packing them up?" asked Benny.

"Oh, they often do that," replied John. "They build steamboats for California, I have heard, to sail on the rivers there, and take them all to pieces and carry them

round in large ships, by sea, and then
put them together again when they get
there."

So saying, John took the sails off the
masts, and the masts out of the vessels,
and then laying the three vessels together,
one upon the top of the other, he put the
sails upon them, spreading them out smooth,
and finally placed the three masts, side by
side, upon the sails. Then he wrapped the
whole up carefully in a large newspaper,
which he took off from a shelf in his cupboard, and tied the parcel securely with a
twine.

"There!" said he, "to-morrow morning
we will put that under one of the seats in
the carriage."

All this time the thunder-shower had
been running its usual course, for it had
been lightening and thundering and raining all the time. The boys had, however,
been so much interested in their work, that
they paid very little attention to the weather,
except that now and then, when the lightning was unusually vivid, Benny would
say, "That was a bright flash!" Other
than this they took very little notice of the

weather without, but gave all their attention to their ship-building.

They now, however, went to the door,
and they found that the shower had nearly
passed by. It was still raining a little, it
is true, but the whole western sky was
nearly clear. The sun, just breaking into
view, was shining brightly among the fall-
ing drops; and though there was a dark
and heavy cloud spreading all over the
eastern sky, the gloom of it was changed
into gladness by the gorgeous colors of a
double rainbow.

CHAPTER XVII.

SAILING THE SHIPS.

THE next morning at breakfast, Mrs. Gay informed the children that she was going to make her excursion that day, the rain having effectually laid the dust, and made the country everywhere look so fresh and green.   So she authorized John and Benny to make arrangements with Wilmot for harnessing the horses into the carryall, and bringing them to the door. They were to be ready at ten o'clock.

John and Benny went out together into the garden, to find Wilmot, and after giving him the necessary directions, they were coming back to the house, when John suddenly turned to look up towards the vane, saying, —

" We must look and see how the wind is, Benny, so as to know whether it is fair for our vessels.   It is south."

" And will that be fair for the vessels ? " asked Benny.

" That depends upon which side of the pond the tavern is, where we are going to stop," replied John. " We will ask mother when we go in. If it is on the south side, it will be all right, for then the wind will blow the vessels directly off the shore, out toward the middle of the pond."

The boys accordingly asked their mother, but she said she did not know much about the points of the compass, and could not tell. All she knew was that the back side of the house was all shady in the middle of the day, and the back side was toward the pond.

If Mrs. Gay had reflected a little, she might have inferred from this that the house was on the south side of the pond. For the shadows of a house are always on the north side of it, in the middle of the day. Of course the back side of the house must have been the north side of it, and as that side of the house was toward the pond, the pond must have been north of the house; or, in other words, the house must have been south of the pond.

When the carryall came to the door, and they were putting in the things, John brought his parcel, to put under the seat.

"Johnny, my boy!" said his mother, "what is that?"

"Some ships," said John. "It is a fleet of ships, — or at least a squadron."

Wilmot stood near the horses' heads until the party were all in, and then gave the reins into John's hands, for he was to be the driver. John was rather a small boy to drive two horses, but then he was a very careful boy, and the horses were well trained.

The carryall had seats for four inside, besides two in front. John and Benny took the two front seats, and Mrs. Gay went inside. On the way they called for Mary and Luly, who were to go too. They got in with Mrs. Gay, and then there were three inside.

The party then set out, and as soon as the carriage was well out of town, Luly and Mary kneeled up upon their seat, turning their faces forward so that they could look out over John's and Benny's shoulders, and see the road and the horses, and everything before them. They liked this way of riding very much.

"Now, children," said Mrs. Gay, "I leave

it to you to regulate the speed as you please. It is ten miles out to the pond, and ten miles back. The faster you drive, of course, the sooner we shall get through our excursion and be at home again."

" Then, John," said Mary, " let us drive very slow."

" Yes," said John ; " I'll let the horses trot along just as they please."

So John put away the whip in its socket, and left the horses pretty much to themselves. They were, however, in excellent spirits, and they trotted along together at a very good rate, turning their heads now and then toward one another, with a knowing look, which seemed to say, " This is just what we like."

Before long, Mary spied a large flock of sheep coming along the road. As they came nearer, she perceived that they filled up the whole road, from side to side, completely.

" Johnny ! " said she, " now how are you going to get by all these sheep ? There is not room for even a wheelbarrow to get through."

" I am not going to get by them at all,"

12

said John. " I am going to let them get by me."

So saying, John, having now come near to the head of the flock, stopped the horses, and let them stand still in the middle of the road, while the sheep — with an infinite deal of crowding and pushing, some of them even getting jammed together about the wheels of the carriage, and under the horses' heels — after a time succeeded in all getting by ; and then John drove on.

The man who was driving the sheep nodded to John as he passed, and said, " Thank you, sir." He thanked him for waiting patiently and giving the sheep time to get by in their own way, instead of trying to drive through them, and so perhaps hurting some of them.

The party travelled on in this way by a winding road, through a very pleasant country, for about two hours ; and then, at last, they came to Warner's tavern, which stood near the shore of Warner's pond. Just before they came to the tavern, there was a broad open space leading down to the shore of the pond, where people travelling along the road could drive down and water their horses.

John drove the carriage up to the door of the tavern, and immediately a man came from a stable on the other side of the way to take the horses, while John helped his mother out of the carriage. Mrs. Gay had a book in her hand, and a small portfolio. The landlady came to the door to receive Mrs. Gay, and conducted her and the children to a very pleasant back room, very neatly and prettily furnished, and with a very comfortable rocking-chair at one of the windows which looked out upon the pond.

"Ah!" exclaimed Mrs. Gay, "this is exactly the place for me."

So she went and took her seat in the rocking-chair, laying her book and her portfolio down upon a table near her. Then she took out her watch.

"Now, children," said she, " it is twelve o'clock. We shall not have dinner till one. So you may go down to the pond, and play for an hour. When it is time for you to come in to dinner, I will ring the bell, or else come and tell you. I think I shall come and tell you."

So the boys, taking the parcel which con-

tained their vessels, set off for the pond.
They went out through an open door at the
end of the entry, which led to a yard, and
thence into a garden.   At the foot of the
garden was a gate, and passing through the
gate the boys came at once to the shore of
the pond.

Here they found a very small but stout
and fat boy engaged in throwing stones
into the water.   They asked him what his
name was, and he said it was Tubby. They
asked him what his other name was, and
he said he had not any other name.   They
asked him where he lived.   He did not answer in words, but pointed to the tavern.

John then proceeded to untie his parcel,
— Benny, Mary, Luly, and Tubby standing by and looking on, — and then proceeded to fit the masts and sails to the several vessels.   There was a gentle breeze,
and the first one they set off was carried
along very smoothly and prettily, out into
the pond.   After she had gone off a little
way from the land, so as to make it impossible that she could be recovered, they all
concluded to play that she was a pirate, or
an enemy, and they began to cannonade

her with stones which they picked up upon the beach.

Their fire, however, as it seems, was not very accurate, for the vessel escaped being hit, and sailed slowly off out over the surface of the pond, the sail growing smaller and smaller all the time, until it was finally lost to view.

It so happened that there was a rocky point, projecting out into the water, at some distance along the shore from where the boys were standing, and the vessel in going out to sea, as John called it, passed not very far from that point.

" Benny," said John, " I wish we had rudders to our vessels, for if we had I believe I could steer them so that they would go to that point, and you and Mary could go and take them in there, and then set them a-sailing again. I could send you something for cargo."

This idea seemed to please the children very much, and John said he could make some rudders out of a shingle if he had one, and if he had a gimlet or something to bore a hole with up through the stern of the vessel to put the stern-rudder through.

He asked Tubby whether there were any shingles about the house, and Tubby said yes; and then he asked him if there was a gimlet, and he said no.

However, they all went to the house to see. Tubby found plenty of shingles, and from one of these John made three very good rudders. Each rudder consisted of a thin blade, to take effect upon the water, and a round stem projecting from it upward, which was intended to be inserted in a hole which was to be made at the stern of the vessel, provided a gimlet could be found to make it.

But there was no gimlet to be found. Tubby took the boys to what he called the shop; but there was nothing there but some remains of an old plough, some broken chains, and a bench with a box of old iron upon it.

"Stop," said John, as his eye fell upon the old iron; "perhaps I can find something here that will do."

So he looked into the box and soon seized upon a pretty stout iron wire, about a foot long, very rusty and crooked at one end.

" This will do," said he, " if they will
only let me heat it red-hot at the kitchen-
fire. Then I can burn the holes out, and
that will do just as well as to bore them."

So they all went to the kitchen, though
Tubby said it would not do any good, for
Patience, the girl who was at work there,
was very cross. Tubby proved to be right,
for when John appeared at the door and
asked leave to heat his wire at the kitchen-
fire, she said, " No, indeed!" If there was
anything she hated, she said, it was to
have children poking about her kitchen-fire.

" Then will you give us some matches?"
asked John, " and we will build a fire for
ourselves down by the pond."

" Yes," said Patience, " I'll give you
three matches if you'll go off and not let
me see your faces here again."

So John took the matches, and they all
went together, carrying the matches and
the wire down to the shore, and there they
built a fire of sticks upon a flat stone, in
which John soon heated his wire so as to
burn the holes. The stems of the rudders
fitted into the holes very well, but before
they got ready to sail the vessels, Mrs. Gay
came down to call them up to dinner.

After dinner they went back and sailed the two remaining vessels very successfully. By means of the rudders, John succeeded in steering them so that they went to the point, and there Mary and Benny received them. Luly remained with John to set the vessels off. The cargoes consisted of some little round cakes which they brought from the dinner-table, and also of some raisins and almonds.

When the two vessels had both been dispatched, John and Luly went to the point, and there, after receiving the vessels when they came into port, they ate up the cargoes, and then set the vessels off again on their long voyage across the pond. They watched them as they sailed away until they disappeared from view, and I believe that none of the three were ever afterward heard from.

The party set out on their return home that afternoon at half past three o'clock, and they had a very pleasant ride. It was a pretty long ride too, for John, in order to protract the pleasure as much as possible, drove so slowly that they did not reach home till after five o'clock.

CHAPTER XVIII.

THE KITE–SHIP.

MARY and Benny were so much pleased with the success of the ship-building operation, and John himself was so much gratified at having been able to afford them such a degree of pleasure by the exercise of his mechanical skill, that he determined that he would make some more vessels the next time they went to Warner's Pond, and in reflecting upon the subject he happened to think of a very curious experiment to try — which he did try, and which succeeded admirably.

He had read somewhere in a book that Dr. Franklin once made a kite, and then went into the water a-swimming, with the kite-string in his hand, — having of course first sent the kite up into the air, — and as soon as he was afloat in the water the kite drew him along on the surface of it, and in this way he was wafted, or rather towed, entirely across the pond.

"In this way," said John, in explaining this subject to Mary, "a real ship might be taken across the Atlantic Ocean, if they could only make a kite big enough, and if the wind would only blow steady in the right direction all the time. I am going to try the experiment myself the next time we go to Warner's Pond."

"No," said Mary, "you must n't do it."

Mary thought that John's plan was to be towed across the pond himself, by the kite, as Dr. Franklin had been. But John explained to her that that was not what he meant. He was going to make a large ship, he said, and send that across the pond, and make believe that it was a ship sailing across the Atlantic by means of a kite instead of sails.

In this form Mary had no objection to the experiment, and so the plan was agreed upon, and the work was at once commenced.

John concluded not to make the vessel itself at home in his shop, but only the masts and rigging for it, as he wished to have a vessel of such a size that it could not be conveniently taken in the carriage.

He accordingly made some tall masts ; the longest was nearly three feet long, and about as large round as a bowsprit. He made a streamer for the top of the principal mast, and some large sails, of stiff white paper.

" But, John," said Mary, " you don't need any sails for your ship. It is to go by the kite instead of by sails."

" True," said John ; " but the people will take sails too, in case of an accident to the kite. They always have sails in steamships, in case of any accident to the engines."

John also prepared some pieces of twine for the rigging, and a hammer, and with it some small nails to drive into different places in his vessel to fasten the rigging to, and a suitable borer to bore holes for the masts. He made a bowsprit too, and fastened a piece of twine, with a loop in the end of it, to the part of the bowsprit which was to be nailed to the vessel. This loop was to fasten the end of the kite-twine to, in order that the kite might draw the vessel along.

John then proceeded to make the kite,

which he said must be very light and very small.

"Oh, no!" said Benny; "make it very large and strong, so that it can pull the vessel along fast."

"Ah! that won't do," said John. "The kite must be so small that it can't pull the vessel along fast, for if the vessel goes fast the kite will come down. Don't you know that if you run fast *toward* your kite when you are holding the string, that it will immediately begin to come down?"

"Yes," said Benny.

"And, on the contrary," added John, "if you turn round and run the other way, then it immediately begins to go up higher?"

"Yes," said Benny.

"So, you see," continued John, "a kite can only be kept up by being held back pretty well. Now as I can't make my ship *very* large, I must make the kite very small, so that a moderately sized ship can hold it back. Besides that, I mean to load the vessel as heavily as I can with stones."

John made his kite about a foot long. He planed down the sticks for the frame until they were exceedingly thin and slender, and instead of twine to bind the parts of the frame together he used thread. He covered it also with tissue-paper. This made the whole structure very light indeed.

For twine to raise his kite by, and attach it to the vessel, he procured a spool of cotton thread. His mother gave him one which she said was marked two hundred yards.

" That will send the kite up very high," said John.

" How high ? " asked Benny.

" Why, two hundred yards, of course," replied John.

" And how high is that ? " asked Benny.

" Five or six times as high as the steeple of a church," replied John.

Benny looked up into the air and endeavored to form a conception in his mind how high that would be. He saw a small white cloud floating at a vast altitude in the sky, and he thought that five or six times as high as the steeple of a church must be at least as high as that cloud.

After John had finished his kite, and had got everything ready, he said that there was one thing more to be done, and that was to write a letter to the consignee.

" What is the consignee ? " asked Benny.

" He is the man," replied John, " that the vessel is sent to. When they send a ship to a foreign country they always send a letter with her to the consignee, to tell him what to do with the cargo."

So John wrote a letter. It was addressed to the person, whoever he might be, who should find the vessel when it should reach the farther shore. It was as follows : —

" Whoever finds this vessel may know that it sailed across the pond by a kite, and if he follows the string along over the land I suppose he will find the kite itself, lying on the ground ; and I wish he would send it up again, when the wind blows the contrary way, and so make the ship sail back again to Warner's tavern."

When Mrs. Gay heard of this plan, and saw all the preparations that John had made, she became quite interested in the idea, and said that she had a great desire to see for herself how the experiment would succeed. Accordingly, before long she arranged a new excursion to Warner's Pond, and there John carried his scheme into effect. He made his vessel of a board about four feet long, — hewing off the corners at one end with an axe to form the bows. He put in the masts, and set up the rigging, and spread the great white sail. He also put the letter on board, and a number of stones for ballast. Then he raised the kite, and, attaching the end of the string to the loop which he had made for it, he set it off on its voyage.

His mother and all the rest of the party stood on a high place on the shore near by and watched it as it sailed slowly away. As they watched it they looked alternately at the kite soaring in the air, and at the vessel moving over the water. They continued to see the sail long after the vessel itself and the kite had disappeared from view.

I have no doubt that the vessel successfully accomplished its voyage, and went entirely across the pond. But whether any of the boys that lived on that side found it there, and set it out on its return voyage, I never learned.

The outward voyage was accomplished successfully, at any rate, and not only the other children, but Mrs. Gay herself, and even Patience, who came down to the foot of the garden to witness it, were very much entertained and amused. In these and in similar ways John found that the knowledge that he had acquired of practical mechanics enabled him to contribute a great deal to the amusement and enjoyment of those around him.

www.ingramcontent.com/pod-product-compliance
Lightning Source LLC
Chambersburg PA
CBHW030550040726
47497CB00008B/2659